WILD RESCUERS

SENTINELS IN THE DEEP OCEAN

Stacy Hinojosa aka *Stacy Plays*

ILLUSTRATED BY Vivienne To

HARPER
An Imprint of HarperCollinsPublishers

Photos on pages 193–194 are courtesy of the author. Photos on pages 197–202 are courtesy of Chelsea Frost (Cape Eleuthera Institute), Steve Hudson (OceanX), Megan McCall (Bayside Academy), Sophie Mills (Cape Eleuthera Institute), and Laura St. Andrews (Cape Eleuthera Institute).

For my dad, Papa Ford, and Grandpapa

CONTENTS

WILD RESCUERS

SENTINELS
IN THE
DEEP OCEAN

Everest

Wink

Stacy

Basil

Tucker

Addison

Noah

Page

Milquetoast

Pipsqueak

Molly

The Mesa Pack

RUNE KEY

A B C D E F G

H I J K L M N

O P Q R S T U

V W X Y Z

ONE

STACY PACED BACK and forth across the cave. A few hours had passed since Everest, the alpha wolf in her pack, brought the sickly lynx cub to Stacy's attention. The cub, Pipsqueak, an orphan they'd rescued from the high mountains that lay north of the taiga, was in very poor condition. Stacy wasn't sure what the weight of a baby lynx ought to be, but Pipsqueak seemed to be very undernourished—the result of being stranded in the snow with no mother for several hours, if not days. Stacy and her pack of wolves had found him just in time. They'd brought him back to their home in the taiga forest and warmed him up, but the cub was refusing food and water. *That's not a good sign,* Stacy thought to herself.

Pipsqueak wasn't the only animal in the cave who was feeling under the weather. Stacy's wolf Tucker was also not well. He was still recovering from transferring a large amount of healing energy to the elder wolf the pack had encountered during their last expedition. It had been in vain—the elder wolf had passed away, leaving Tucker weakened and inconsolable. Stacy had set Addison, the brainiest wolf in her pack, in charge of tending to Tucker, and tasked Noah, her blue-eyed wolf, with watching over Pipsqueak while she and the others attended to another animal who needed rescuing in the taiga. It had turned out to be a false alarm— an old opossum who was playing . . . well, who had been pretending to be asleep. Stacy had rushed back to Pipsqueak's side and had been there ever since—pacing about and consulting the small library of books she had in the cave, trying to figure out what was wrong with him.

"If his condition doesn't improve by morning, I'm going to have to take him to the animal hospital in the village," Stacy said to her wolves, who were milling about the cave. Noah was changing out the cub's small water bowl, using the tiny stream at the back of the cave to fetch fresh water for Pipsqueak. Addison was ladling out pumpkin stew to Everest and Basil, who were eagerly lapping it up. And Wink and Tucker were lying in front of the hearth. Page and Molly, Stacy's rescue dogs, were also near the fire, which cracked and popped as the evening stretched on. Stacy walked over to where Pipsqueak and her cat Milquetoast were nestled and scratched Milquetoast under his chin.

"Such a good big brother," she cooed. Next, Stacy gently stroked Pipsqueak's back. She knew there was an animal hospital in town, but it was mostly for the livestock from the farms that surrounded the village— animals like cows, pigs, sheep, and horses. Stacy wasn't sure what they would say if she were to stroll in with a lynx cub. She would need to come up with a convincing story to tell . . . as well as money to pay for whatever medicine Pipsqueak required.

I think I have some money lying around here. Stacy walked over to her bookshelf and rummaged around, searching for any spare coins or bills she had tucked either between her books on the lower shelf or on the top shelf where Fluff, her chicken, roosted. She gathered every bit of change she could find and spread it out on her desk to count.

"Five dollars and nineteen cents," Stacy counted.

"That's probably not enough." Stacy had long thought she should get a part-time job in the village—perhaps washing dishes at the village diner where her only human friend, Miriam, worked. Stacy visited her at the diner nearly every week and had gotten a lot better at speaking to other humans since she first met Miriam in the taiga almost a year ago. Stacy knew having a bit of money around was a smart idea—she could use it to buy food during the cold winter months when things were scarce, or to purchase seeds for Addison to plant or occasional treats for her and her animals (like jars of peanut butter), or for instances like this when one of her pets needed medicine. Stacy had come to rely on Tucker being able to heal any injury or sickness that anyone in the group had. None of them knew yet if his powers would return. But even if they didn't, Tucker was still a very good natural healer and knew the best herbal remedies growing around the forest. That knowledge wouldn't go away, at least. *Even if I were to get a part-time job, though, there's still the problem of people asking why I'm not in school. What would I tell them?*

As for Stacy's other wolves, their powers were still very much intact. Basil was as fast as ever. Wink was indestructible. Everest could read Stacy's thoughts and camouflage into the forest. Noah could hold his breath underwater for as long as he wanted, and Addison possessed human-like intelligence. *Actually, Addison is smarter than most humans. At least . . . this human anyhow.* It had been Addison who brought Stacy books to read when she was younger and instilled a love of reading and writing in her. Stacy looked down at the two diaries on her desk. One was her own—filled with stories of the animal rescues she and her pack had performed in the taiga over the years. The other was the one she'd found in the cavern in the glacier on the tundra a few days ago. It was written in code—code that Addison knew how to read perfectly. Stacy was still learning.

This much Stacy knew: the diary had belonged to a female Arctic explorer who, like Stacy, had discovered wolves with powers. For years, she had lived in hiding with a pair of wolves—Stacy's wolves' parents—in a cavern on the tundra, studying the wolves' behavior and protecting the secret of their existence. But something had gone wrong, because when Stacy found the cavern, only the old male wolf was there, and he died soon after. Stacy didn't know where the explorer was now, but she was grateful she had this journal that she could translate. She also had a mysterious rune she had copied down from the explorer's base that she had finished decoding only a few hours ago. Translated, it read:

Stacy struggled to make sense of the rune. There were words she recognized. *Tundra. Taiga. Mesa.* Stacy had been to all three of those biomes and guessed that the explorer had too. Other words she knew—words like *amethyst* and *diamond*—but didn't understand what they meant in relation to the three biomes. And then there were words Stacy didn't recognize at all. *Lqcca. Auiom. Patpb. Irrpe.* Stacy hadn't a clue what those words meant, but she desperately wanted to understand. She wanted to read the journal in its entirety and secretly wondered if someday she would be able to read and write in the code language like Addison and the explorer. But until that day came, she would have to translate each letter by hand, which was a slow and arduous task. And one that would have to wait until Pipsqueak was better. He needed Stacy's full attention right now.

Stacy walked to the entrance of the cave and poked her head out. Even though it was still dark, she could just barely make out the shapes of the towering spruce trees that surrounded their little cave—a sign that morning's first light would soon reach them. Suddenly, there was a commotion behind Stacy. She spun around to see Everest, Basil, Addison, Wink, Noah, Page, and Molly all getting to their feet. Instantly, Stacy saw what had their attention—Tucker was standing!

Tucker walked slowly to the back of the cave and took a long drink from the stream. Then he turned to face the others, water still dripping from his muzzle, and they all ran over to him, meeting him with enthusiastic tail wagging and head nuzzles. Tucker greeted each of them, almost smiling. Stacy knew wolves didn't really smile, but Tucker's cheery disposition made it seem like he was. Stacy realized how gloomy the cave had seemed while Tucker was recovering. Now that he could move on his own again, everything suddenly felt brighter. Stacy was sure the cave had gotten ten degrees warmer. She ran over to him and threw her arms around the massive white wolf.

"Tucker!" Stacy breathed into his fur. "I'm so happy you're okay."

Stacy gripped Tucker's thick fur with her fingers and pulled herself closer to him.

"Addison," Stacy said, turning to her spectacled wolf. "Will you make something for Tucker to eat, please?"

Addison nodded and walked over to the small kitchen in the cave. Meanwhile, Tucker strode confidently toward Pipsqueak.

"Tucker, maybe you'd better not . . ." Stacy started. But Tucker was already pressing his head to Pipsqueak, determined to heal him from whatever infection or ailment he had.

Seconds passed. And then a full minute. Pipsqueak didn't stir.

"It's okay," Stacy said to Tucker, whose face bore a forlorn expression. "It's not you. He's too sick. He needs a doctor."

Stacy wasn't entirely sure if that was true or if Tucker really *had* lost his ability to heal other animals. But she didn't want Tucker to feel bad. Stacy scooped up Pipsqueak and tucked him gently into her leather satchel and slung it over her shoulders. She layered her flannel sleeping shirt over the blue-and-white-striped, long-sleeve T-shirt she was wearing, since the sun was still on its way up in the sky.

"I'm heading to the village," Stacy announced to the others. "Hopefully the animal hospital will be open by the time I get there."

Stacy said good-bye to Page, Molly, and Milquetoast—giving each of them a pat on the head and a small biscuit from the batch Addison had just whipped up. Then Stacy and Everest headed out of the cave and west toward the river that divided the taiga from the farms that surrounded the village.

I don't want to hear it, Everest, Stacy thought as she trudged through the taiga. She knew Everest could hear what she was thinking—it was the first power he had developed, and, to Stacy, it was both a blessing and a curse. It was a blessing because Stacy could instantly communicate with Everest, even if he was far away, which made animal rescues easier. But it was a curse because it meant that Everest knew everything Stacy was thinking before she had a chance to explain some of her crazier schemes. For instance, Stacy knew that Everest hadn't been too thrilled when she brought home her first cat, Milquetoast. And now a big cat? Definitely not. A lynx would grow to be at least fifty pounds in size. *We don't even know if this little guy is going to make it, Everest. We've got to be prepared for the worst. But we couldn't have left him alone on that mountain to freeze to death! We did the right thing in rescuing him.*

Everest nodded in agreement as he walked alongside Stacy. Stacy knew this was the best response she was going to get from him. She also knew that Everest was only trying to protect her and the others. The truth was that caring for a lynx was way beyond Stacy's abilities. She wasn't sure how she was going to manage it. She also wasn't sure how she was going to pay for Pipsqueak to see a village doctor, but she trusted that it would all work out . . . somehow.

Stacy and Everest crossed the river, which was moving fast due to all the melting snow from the mountains that lay north of the taiga. Light was just beginning to shine on the dewy farmland that surrounded the village. Stacy and Everest walked briskly across the first pasture, which was filled with grazing cattle.

Stacy reached inside her satchel and cupped the little cub's head. He didn't move at all. "Hang on just a little longer, okay? We're going to get you help."

Stacy and Everest had just hopped over a wooden fence and started up a hill filled with sheep when she saw the farmer staring at them, his mouth hanging open. He reached for something that was hanging at his side—a rifle—and slowly and shakily raised it up to point at them.

"Stop right there . . . or I'll shoot."

TWO

"WHAT IN THE world do you think you're doing?" the
farmer shouted at Stacy. "I saw you walking with that
wolf!" Stacy froze in shock. The farmer spun around,
his rifle still raised.

"Where did he go?" he said frantically. "I just saw
him."

Stacy turned around to discover that Everest was no
longer standing beside her. She began to panic. *I knew
Everest coming with me was a bad idea. He could get shot!
And Tucker isn't here to heal him—and might not be able
to heal him even if he was. Everest . . . where are you?*

Suddenly, Stacy realized what Everest had done. *He's*

using his camouflage ability! He must be around here some-
where . . . hiding in plain sight. Stacy scanned the horizon
once more and spotted him instantly—concealed among
the flock of sheep, his white fur easily blending in with
their white fleece. It was the kind of thing you could
only see if you were expecting to see a nearly invisible
wolf standing in front of you. But the farmer would
never suspect it. Stacy knew what she had to do. She
turned back toward the farmer.

"A wolf?" Stacy said innocently. "Oh no! Where? I
haven't seen any wolves. I was just admiring your sheep
over there." Stacy knew pointing to the sheep was risky,
but she also had to convince the farmer that he was hal-
lucinating.

"What?" the farmer said. "No, there was a huge wolf
here a second ago. And I read something in the paper
a few months back about a white wolf in the forest. I
could have sworn I saw. . ."

"I'm sorry, mister," Stacy interrupted him. "But you
think that I was in your field with a white wolf? And the
wolf didn't frighten your flock?"

The farmer lowered his rifle and furrowed his brow.
"I know what I saw," he said, sounding less convinced
than he was before. "I swear I saw what I saw. . . ."

Stacy felt bad lying to the old man. But she knew it

was for his own good. She walked up to him and put her arm on his.

"Sir?" Stacy said sweetly. "Are you feeling okay?"

"I . . . I must not be," the old man stammered, blinking several times and shaking his head. "I just could have sworn . . ."

Stacy turned the man toward the village and started walking with him. "You should probably lie down," she said. "And then maybe have something to eat. But before you do that, would you mind pointing me in the direction of the village animal doctor?" Stacy looked back to see a relieved-looking Everest trotting home toward the taiga. It wasn't like Everest to slip up when it came to humans—Stacy was sure he hadn't been expecting to see anyone out this early. She couldn't wait to tell the others when she got home about Everest's close brush with the farmer. Hopefully he wouldn't be too sheepish about it.

"Oh, you mean the veterinarian?" the farmer asked Stacy, snapping her back to the present. "Her office is on the west side of the village. If you take a left at the diner and walk about a quarter mile, you'll run straight into it."

Stacy had no idea what the word *veterinarian* meant, but she knew where the diner was.

"Thank you so much," she said. "I hope you get to feeling better." But what she really meant was that she hoped the farmer believed he'd imagined it all and didn't tell anyone about what he'd seen.

The farmer nodded and started toward his farmhouse.

"Happy to help," he said. "I'm just glad there wasn't a wolf. Imagine that. I must have been seeing things."

Stacy waved good-bye, relieved she had been able to convince the farmer that he hadn't seen Everest. She headed down the dirt lane, away from the farmer's house and toward the village. She made her way to the diner and peered through the window. She could see Miriam setting up tables for the breakfast rush. Stacy thought about popping in to say good morning, but she knew the little cub needed a doctor straightaway. Besides, Stacy wasn't sure she wanted to tell Miriam about the cub. Miriam was keeping Stacy's secret: that she lived in the taiga with wolves. But a wild lynx? That might be too much for Miriam to understand.

Stacy headed west and quickened her pace. Soon enough, she arrived at the doctor's office. It was open! Stacy pushed the door in and stepped inside.

"Welcome, do you have an appointment?" a cheery woman asked Stacy from behind a desk. Stacy steeled herself. She still wasn't used to lying, even though she had to every time she visited the village. *I'm going to need to lie about my name, where I'm from, and how I rescued this animal . . . I might as well be honest about everything else.*

"I'm sorry, I don't," Stacy said. "I don't have much money either, but I found this lynx cub while I was hiking in the forest and he's very sick."

Stacy reached into her satchel and pulled Pipsqueak out and showed him to the woman.

"Oh dear, poor thing does look to be in bad shape," the woman said. "We'll get you right in to see the doctor, just have a seat over there for a moment. And don't worry about payment, I'm sure we'll be able to work something out."

She motioned to a small waiting area to the left of where her desk was. Stacy took a seat and looked around at the walls. They were filled with framed posters. Two of them were charts of different dog and cat breeds. Another explained which foods were unsafe for pets to consume. *Grapes . . . garlic . . . onions . . . good to know,* Stacy thought.

She looked down at the coffee table in front of where she was sitting and saw an array of veterinary journals and pet magazines. She picked one up and began flipping through the pages. *What a cool job it must be to be a . . .*

veterinarian, she thought, taking a second to remember the word. *I bet it requires a lot of schooling—I've never even been to school. Although . . . Tucker is sort of like a veterinarian. I bring him sick or hurt animals from around the taiga, and he makes them better! Our cave is like our office . . . and Milo the bat is our receptionist!*

"The doctor will see you now . . . er, what did you say your name was again?" the woman said to Stacy. Stacy jerked her head up to meet the woman's gaze.

"Daisy," Stacy said. "My name is Daisy."

It was a lie Stacy didn't feel too bad about telling. She didn't think it was smart to use her real name. After all, her parents had gone missing while piloting a helicopter. They had never been found, and somehow Stacy had survived. Stacy had been living with the wolves since then, but that didn't mean that there hadn't been an airport with a flight manifest, or some type of record to show that Stacy had been a passenger as well. Stacy thought it best to use a fake name, and Daisy sort of sounded like Stacy anyway.

"All right, Daisy," the woman said. "Right this way."

Stacy pushed through a heavy iron door into a hallway with several other doors. The woman guided her through the second door they came to. Inside were a chair, a tall metal table, a round stool on wheels, and a small counter with a sink and a cabinet above it. The room felt cold and bare, and Stacy began to wonder if coming here had been a good idea after all.

But before Stacy could worry too much about what she had gotten herself and Pipsqueak into, there was a soft knock on the door, and the doctor walked in. She was short and stocky and had stick-straight hair the same tawny color as the pebbles on the shore of the river in the taiga. She was dressed in a white jacket and a pair of khaki trousers and had a strange silver instrument draped around her neck. She wore a watch on her left wrist, and a pair of sturdy and well-worn leather boots poked out from her trousers, as if she'd spent the morning in a horse stable or in a pasture with farm animals. She looked Stacy directly in the eyes and smiled.

"Hello, Daisy, I'm Dr. Kay!" she said.

Stacy managed a feeble hello to Dr. Kay. She immediately felt intimidated by her. Stacy hoped she'd be able to find her voice to get Pipsqueak the help he needed.

"This lynx is sick," Stacy said quietly, pulling Pipsqueak from her satchel and setting him on the tall metal table.

"Lynx?" Dr. Kay exclaimed. "This looks like a house cat to me!"

Dr. Kay scooped Pipsqueak up and placed him on a small scale on the table.

"Two and a half pounds . . ." she said in a worried tone. "That does seem small for his age."

She peered inside Pip's small mouth, curling his little lip upward so she could inspect his teeth and gums.

"I would guess he's around twelve weeks old," she said to Stacy. "He needs to eat—what have you been feeding him?"

Stacy felt the emotions inside her begin to bubble to the surface. Suddenly, it all came rushing out of her.

"He's not eating anything!" Stacy said. "He's not drinking either, and I don't know what to do. I only found him the other day, and I tried to feed him a little bit of salmon, but he's just not interested."

Dr. Kay reached up to her neck. She brought the strange device she was wearing up to her ears and held the small, round metal disk at the opposite end of it. She pressed it against Pipsqueak's chest and closed her eyes.

"Um," Stacy said. "Can I ask what you're doing?"

Dr. Kay's eyes opened, and she looked at Stacy.

"I'm using my stethoscope . . ." she explained. "Hasn't a doctor used one on you at one of your checkups?"

Stacy instantly regretted saying something. *Of course*

this office would be filled with things Stacy *should* recognize. Doctors' offices for animals and humans must not be that different from one another.

"Oh, um," Stacy stammered. "I don't remember."

"This is my stethoscope—it lets me listen to his heartbeat," Dr. Kay said. "Here, give it a try."

Stacy put the stethoscope in her ears and immediately heard the soft rhythm of a heartbeat. Pipsqueak closed his eyes and started to purr. Stacy was amazed. She had no idea how the stethoscope worked, but she was in awe of Dr. Kay and her ability to help animals. Stacy took the stethoscope out of her ears and handed it back to the doctor.

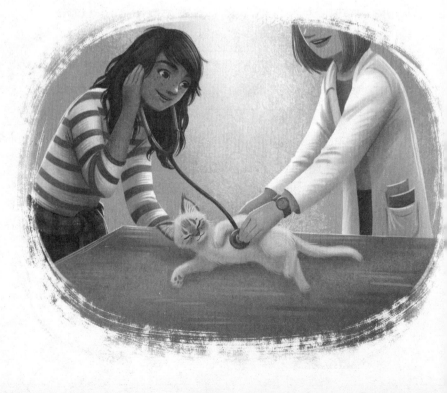

"Is Pipsqueak going to be okay?" Stacy asked.

Dr. Kay paused and looked concerned. "I'd like to run some tests on him to determine what the issue is," she said. "It should only take an hour, and you can come back and pick him up then."

Stacy nodded. She didn't love the idea of leaving Pipsqueak at the animal hospital, but she also knew that he was in good hands with Dr. Kay and that this was his best chance of survival.

Stacy gave Pipsqueak a kiss on the top of his head and left the room. She exited the animal hospital and headed toward the diner where Miriam worked. Stacy figured she could stop in and visit her and maybe even have something to eat for breakfast while she waited for Pipsqueak to finish his tests.

Stacy was scared that Pipsqueak's tests would reveal bad news, but she tried to remain optimistic. And she was happy to be heading toward the diner. Stacy loved visiting Miriam (and getting a free meal) and went as often as possible. Miriam had been the one who tipped Stacy off about the team of researchers who were tracking the taiga wolves just a few weeks ago. Because of that information, Stacy and her pack knew to leave the taiga for a bit—for an expedition on the tundra—to evade the researchers. It wasn't that Stacy didn't like the head researcher, Dr. Berg, and his team of students. Quite the contrary—Stacy knew that studying wolves was actually what was in the wolves' best interest. The more that humans learned about wolf behavior, the better the villagers near the taiga would understand that wolves weren't a threat but should be left alone and treated with respect. But Stacy's wolves couldn't be studied—not with their supernatural powers. Everest's telepathy and invisibility . . . Basil's super speed and penchant for pyrotechnics . . . Wink's indestructability . . . Noah's underwater breathing . . . Tucker's healing . . . Addison's super intelligence . . . What would the researchers think about those?

Luckily, Stacy and her wolves had seen the researchers heading north as they were returning to the taiga, so there was nothing to worry about now. But Stacy wondered if Droplet and Splat, the two timber wolves she had rescued and raised last summer, had been collared. . . .

Stacy looked up and realized she had arrived at the village diner just as Miriam was unlocking the door to let in customers.

"Stacy!" Miriam exclaimed. "Good to see you! Come in, come in."

Stacy followed Miriam into the diner and took a seat at the counter on one of the bright red stools.

"What brings you in so early?" Miriam asked her, setting a placemat down for Stacy and handing her a menu. "Here, order some breakfast."

Stacy had never been to the diner for breakfast before and looked at the long menu, unsure of what to order. She settled on the eggs Benedict with asparagus. While she waited for the cook to prepare her breakfast, Stacy caught Miriam up on some of the events that had happened since Stacy was last at the diner—namely, that she had kept the cat she'd found the last time she was in the village, and named him Milquetoast, and that she had found another animal (Pipsqueak) who was currently at the village veterinarian. She decided to leave out the expedition on the tundra. Stacy was grateful that Miriam trusted her to live alone in the taiga with her wolves—she didn't exactly want to tell Miriam about the polar bear encounter she'd had . . . or the avalanche she'd survived only a few days ago.

Stacy's breakfast arrived—two poached eggs on top of two perfectly toasted English muffins, nestled next to a small bundle of steamed asparagus, with a creamy yellow sauce on top, sprinkled with some paprika. Stacy cut into one of the eggs, spilling orangey-yellow yolk onto her plate and over the asparagus. She'd never prepared any of the eggs from her chicken, Fluff, this way before—they were so . . . fluffy, and she couldn't figure out how the chef had done it.

"He cracks them into a pot of boiling water," Miriam said. Stacy realized she must have been staring at her eggs in amazement. Next, she took a bite of the asparagus—the vegetable was cooked to perfection. Stacy had eaten asparagus lots of times before, as it grew wild near the river in the taiga. She'd pick it often in the springtime when she would go fishing with Noah. The sauce was delicious—buttery and creamy with just a hint of lemon. Everything tasted so good together. Stacy wondered if she and Addison could somehow assemble all the ingredients to re-create it sometime.

The diner was busy with villagers coming and going during the hour Stacy was there. She watched as Miriam confidently waited on the different villagers. Stacy was impressed by how Miriam could remember each villager's order and operate the cash register while also remembering when certain villagers needed their coffee mug refilled and others needed their check.

Finally, most of the villagers had paid their checks and left, leaving Miriam to clean up the plates and wipe down the counter.

"Did you like your breakfast?" she asked Stacy while she began brewing a fresh pot of coffee.

"Yes, thank you!" Stacy answered earnestly.

Stacy looked up at the clock and realized it was almost time to pick up Pipsqueak.

"Before you go, Stacy . . ." Miriam said. "I wanted to talk to you about something."

Stacy braced herself for more bad news, but Miriam's expression seemed to soften, and she leaned over and put her hand on Stacy's arm.

"School will be starting up in the fall. . . . I know you have an, um, interesting arrangement in the forest, but I could tell the school that I'm your guardian to sign you up if you wanted. You could go to school."

Stacy took in Miriam's words, but almost couldn't believe she was hearing them correctly. *I could go to school?* Stacy's immediate emotion was one of excitement, followed quickly by fear. She had never been to school . . . at least, she could not remember ever going to school. She was about eight years old when her parents' helicopter crashed in the taiga, killing them and leaving her orphaned and alone in the forest. Luckily, Stacy's pack of wolves had taken her in, but it *was* possible she had attended a year or two of school before that. That would certainly explain how Stacy knew certain things—like how to read and write, and some nursery rhymes, and a few songs about animals. But most of her memories had been erased by the helicopter crash. She had remembered her own name, but that was about it. Stacy couldn't remember anything about her parents, and that made her sad to think about.

All of Stacy's feelings must have registered on her face, because Miriam squeezed Stacy's hand and simply said, "Why don't you take some time to think it over. It's not until the fall, and you have the whole summer in front of you."

"Thank you," Stacy said softly. "Thank you so much, Miriam."

Stacy really meant it too. Even though she wasn't sure whether she would take Miriam up on her generous offer, Stacy realized how meaningful the offer was. *Miriam must think of me almost like family.* Stacy was so grateful for that day last summer when she'd met Miriam in the forest.

"Well, I'd better be getting back to the veterinarian," Stacy said, wiping her mouth and hopping off the bar stool. "Thank you again for breakfast, and I will definitely give your offer a lot of thought."

Stacy's smile faded from her face as soon as she left the diner. On her way back to the animal hospital, she couldn't help but think about what it would be like to attend school with classmates who were her age. Sure,

Stacy had grown up under the tutelage of a super-smart wolf, Addison, but there was no way to know if what she had learned under Addison's watchful eye was what Stacy needed to know to keep up in school. *What if I'm the dumbest one in the whole class?* Stacy had a feeling that, regardless of whatever grade she was in, the lessons would not be centered around the different plants and animals of the taiga forest . . . or confined to the letter *H*, which was the only encyclopedia book Stacy had back in the cave. Still, she had read a lot. Addison had seen to that—bringing Stacy all sorts of different books she'd found in the woods or stolen from the village library book return. But Stacy couldn't help but worry that she wouldn't be able to keep up with her fellow classmates.

Stacy was looking down sullenly at the ground, and so she did not see the large spotted dog running full speed in her direction. The dog collided with Stacy's knees, sending Stacy toppling over. She caught herself with her hands before hitting the cobblestone street. The dog, mostly white but freckled all over with black spots, spun around and sniffed at Stacy. Stacy met the dog's gaze. It looked scared. Suddenly, the dog darted off again, running away down the village streets.

"Hey!" Stacy shouted. "Come back!"

THREE

"IS THIS SOMEONE'S dog?" Stacy called out. She spun her head around in all directions and realized there were no villagers nearby. *The dog must be lost! Normally I'd do this with my wolf pack . . . but it looks like I'm on my own for this rescue!*

Stacy took off after the swift dog as it continued to race through the village. Stacy could barely keep up with it, but something deep inside her caused her legs to run faster. *This must be someone's dog. It's a member of someone's family. What if Page or Molly were lost? I'd want someone to do everything they could to help me get them back.* Stacy trained her eyes on the back of the dog as it ran—its thin white tail swaying back and forth. Stacy didn't know dogs could have as many spots as this dog had. It reminded her of the narwhal, Norman, she had met while journeying across the tundra biome.

Suddenly, Stacy had a thought. She hadn't fully unpacked her satchel from her trip to the tundra, and she had kept some climbing rope in there. . . . *Could it be there still?* Stacy dug her hand into her satchel, a task made more complicated by the fact that she was still running as fast as she could. *Yes!* The rope was still there. Stacy searched for one of the ends, pulled it out, and began to tie a slip knot in it that she could use to toss around the dog's neck. She looked up to see the dog had gained quite a bit of ground on her. Stacy lowered her head and leaned forward, trying to imitate Basil, her fastest wolf, as she ran. The dog was nearing the village bakery, and just as the dog was about to run past it, the door to the bakery swung open and a villager emerged, holding an enormous cake in both hands. It was white and square and had a simple decoration of bright red cherries on top. Before Stacy could open her lips to call out, the dog crashed into the villager. He buckled forward and then backward, throwing his arms up to the sky, launching the cake upward. Stacy watched in horror as the cake flew five feet up in the air before landing at the villager's feet and splattering into pieces. The dog turned to run again but then smelled the cake and began to eagerly eat it off the ground as the villager sobbed.

Stacy took advantage of the opportunity to creep closer to the dog and gently loop her lasso around his neck as he ate.

"There," she said, tightening the knot so her lead was secure. "I got you."

Stacy picked up a piece of the crumbled cake that hadn't touched the cobblestone and took a bite.

"Is that . . . beets?" Stacy asked, still unsure whether she liked the cake's flavor or not.

"Yes," the villager muttered between loud sniffles from his protruding nose. "It was red velvet."

Stacy slowly pulled the dog away from the cake, leaving the villager to clean up the mess. She had no idea how she was going to go about finding the dog's owners. *Everest would kill me if I brought another pet home to the cave.* But it was way past the time to pick up Pipsqueak now, and Stacy figured the animal hospital would be a good place to ask around.

It didn't take long to get to the animal hospital. The dog was a very fast walker, and Stacy was so eager to see Pipsqueak she kept having to stop herself from breaking into a run. She pushed through the doors, making sure the door didn't close on the dog's tail, and entered the animal hospital.

"Well, who is this lovely dalmatian?" the woman behind the counter asked. "Another one of your pets, Daisy?"

"A . . . a what?" Stacy asked.

"A dalmatian!" the woman replied. "That's the breed of dog you're holding. It's known for having black spots all over it, although sometimes they can be brown too. Those are called liver-spotted dalmatians."

"I found him running loose in the village," Stacy said. "I think his owners lost him."

The dalmatian turned around and nuzzled Stacy's knees.

"You should take him next door to the animal shelter then," the woman said. "When you get back, the doctor can meet with you about Pipsqueak. He's doing just fine, by the way. Everyone who works here has fallen in love with him."

The words put Stacy's mind at ease a little. *Does that mean Pipsqueak is going to be okay? Or is she just trying to make me less nervous about getting his test results from Dr. Kay?* Stacy smiled politely and told the woman she'd be back soon. She walked outside and headed toward the next building, which had a sign that read "Village

County Animal Shelter" on it in big black letters.

Nothing could have prepared Stacy for what she saw the moment she stepped inside, still holding the dalmatian on a short lead. In front of her were rows and rows of dogs in cages, each dog more unique than the next. There was a huge black-and-white dog—he didn't have as many spots as the dalmatian did, but the spots he did have were large and stretched across his broad back. A white patch of hair formed a dividing line down his face, and his muzzle had pink and black polka dots around his mouth and on top of his snout. His long tongue hung out of his mouth to one side and, on the other side, a string of drool jiggled and swayed back and forth. Another dog was small like a cat, but she looked almost like a fox kit. She reminded Stacy of a miniature version of Page, with giant pointed ears with wispy tendrils and a streak of black hair down her back. She had a crooked tail that looked like it had been broken at one time and healed funny. It wagged nonstop as she yapped and ran in crazy circles inside her cage. Another dog looked a bit like Molly—tricolor with a light brown face—only she was much leaner and taller and had short hair. Her ears were shorter than Molly's too, as if they used to stick straight up and someone had folded them over. The muscular dog sat in a perfect pose with her front paws

neatly tucked into her haunches. The last dog Stacy saw looked much older than the others. His black-and-white coat was scruffy and wiry, and he was sprawled out on his belly, his pointed snout resting on the cold floor.

Stacy had never seen so many dogs in her life! And they were each so unique. A young man walked along the row of cages over to where Stacy and the dalmatian were standing and introduced himself.

"Hi, I'm Ezra," he said. "Who is this?" He bent down and patted the dalmatian on the head.

"I'm Stacy," Stacy said, before she realized he was talking about the dog.

Stacy decided to use her real name. She was tired of making up stories as she had with the farmer and the receptionist at the animal hospital.

"I found this dog running around in the streets and was told I should bring him here."

"Great!" Ezra replied. "Well, you've definitely brought him to the right place. We take in stray dogs from the village and the surrounding farms and neighborhoods. Any dog who doesn't have a home or has lost their owners is welcome here."

"Why . . . why wouldn't a dog have a home?" Stacy asked. She assumed all dogs who were here had lost their owners and that their owners were out looking for them.

"Sadly, sometimes people will drop dogs off here at our shelter if they don't want them anymore. It could be a case where they didn't get their dog spayed or neutered and it had puppies they can't care for . . . or the dog is bored and chews up their favorite things and they want to get rid of it. Or, in very sad cases, their dog is old and will die soon, and they don't want to have it around anymore."

Stacy bit into her lip to keep from crying.

"There are people who would do that?" she asked Ezra.

"Yes, unfortunately," he replied. "But we are lucky because we have the facilities to take in all the dogs and keep them here until people come to adopt them. That's not the case in every shelter. Sometimes dogs and cats have to be killed in order to make room for all the other dogs and cats they have coming in. Sometimes dogs only have a week or two to get adopted before they are put to sleep permanently . . . even if they are in good health."

"That's . . . horrific," Stacy whispered. She couldn't believe that humans were so selfish and greedy that not only had they tried to take homes away from the animals in the forest by bulldozing the land, but they couldn't even provide good homes for the dogs and cats they had domesticated as pets. *How could they be so cruel?*

"Here, I can take him," Ezra said, placing his own lead around the dog's neck and handing Stacy's rope back to her. "We'll put up some flyers with his picture on them and see if anyone reports him as missing. But if not, he will have a blanket, a toy, and two good meals per day here until he gets adopted. I'm sure a beautiful dog like this will have no problem finding a loving forever home."

"I hope so," Stacy said, giving the dog a hug and a pat on the head.

"A lot of people want purebred dogs like dalmatians," Ezra added. "Personally, I like mixed-breed dogs the best. Mutts are unique."

Mutts? That must be what Page and Molly are. That settles it . . . my favorite breed of dog is a mutt!

"Well, I better go," Stacy said. "My cat is next door at the animal hospital getting checked out."

Ezra nodded. "I hope your cat is okay. And if you ever want to come back—we are always in need of volunteers to help us give the dogs baths, feed them, and exercise them."

"I would love that!" Stacy said as she headed out the door. Stacy smiled. How wonderful if she could spend a few hours before or after her lunches with Miriam helping out at the Village County Animal Shelter. Stacy practically skipped back to the animal hospital, but her excitement faded as she remembered what was about to happen. She would be meeting with the doctor to learn whether Pipsqueak could be saved or not.

Stacy was ushered into the room in the back and waited nervously for several minutes until Dr. Kay entered the room holding Pipsqueak.

"It was just as I suspected," she said enthusiastically, setting Pipsqueak down on the counter. "Pip is not a lynx. He's a regular pet cat!"

"A cat?" Stacy said incredulously. "Like . . . a normal cat?"

"He's definitely going to be on the larger side of domesticated cats," Dr. Kay told Stacy. "I would guess he's a lynx point Siamese mixed with a Maine coon breed."

Stacy took in this information slowly. *If Pipsqueak is just a big cat, that means that he and Milquetoast will be able to play together. And he won't get bigger than Page and Molly. And he won't compete for food with my wolves or want to hunt in the taiga—I'll be able to keep him fed just like Milquetoast with the salmon and trout Noah catches. We will be able to keep him forever in the cave! Unless . . .*

"But is he going to get better?" Stacy asked, looking up at Dr. Kay. "He seemed so sick."

"He was very undernourished, and his little body was beginning to shut down," she said. "You found him just in time. A few more hours and he would not be with us anymore. We've given him some subcutaneous fluids, some standard shots, and some antibiotics. He also has a nasty case of worms in his stomach, but this medicine will clear that right up."

Dr. Kay handed Stacy a bag containing several oral syringes filled with a thick yellow liquid.

"Give him one of those twice a day until you run out, and then his appetite should come back," she said. "In fact, I bet his appetite will be pretty insatiable."

Stacy wasn't entirely sure what that word meant, but she knew one thing for certain, and it was the only thing that mattered to her in that moment: Pip was going to live.

FOUR

STACY SAT AT her desk in the back of the cave and stared at the runes in her journal. It was the next day, and Pipsqueak was already showing signs of improvement. She had been giving him the medicine, and he had slept for a long time, almost the entire night. Everest had woken up with him very early and helped him to take a few bites of pumpkin. It was now late afternoon, and he'd eaten a portion of fish around noon and even showed a few signs of wanting to play with Milquetoast. Stacy hadn't nearly enough money to pay the bill for Pip's care, but Dr. Kay told Stacy she could work off what she owed by helping at the animal hospital in the summer when Stacy wasn't in school. Stacy hadn't bothered to tell Dr. Kay that she didn't go to school. Stacy hadn't decided what to do about Miriam's offer. She still wasn't sure how she really felt about it. She also wasn't sure what Addison would think, and she didn't want to tell any of the wolves just yet, either. She had been trying her hardest not to think about it ever since she got back to the taiga, which had proved impossible. Stacy suspected Everest already knew.

Stacy put the thought out of her mind again and went back to looking at the rune in her journal. *Lqcca. Auiom. Patpb. Irrpe. This has got to be another language that I don't know.* Stacy was frustrated. *If I can't figure this rune out, how am I supposed to go to a school where I don't know anyone and I haven't learned any of the things they've learned? I will definitely be the dumbest one in my class. Maybe Miriam was just trying to be nice.*

Everest walked over from where he was watching Pipsqueak and nuzzled her shoulder. *You must know what I'm thinking about, Everest, but nothing has been decided.* Everest gave her an understanding nod. Just then, Addison walked over to Stacy. The spectacled wolf bent over Stacy's shoulder, looking at the runes. The two of them stared at the page until Stacy's eyes hurt. The unfamiliar shapes all began to blur together for her. Suddenly,

Addison nudged Stacy's shoulder, breaking Stacy from her trance. Stacy looked to Addison, whose eyes were darting around wildly at Stacy's scrawls. Then, Addison took her nose and pressed it to the page of Stacy's journal, dragging it down the letters.

"L . . . a . . . p . . . i . . . s," Stacy read aloud as Addison moved her nose. "Lapis!"

Stacy jumped up from her wooden stool. *I know that word!* Stacy knew lapis lazuli was a deep blue metamorphic rock found in caves. *The words aren't meant to be read horizontally; they're written vertically!*

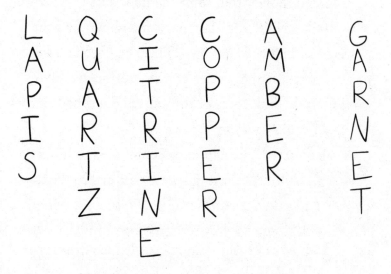

"Addi, you're a genius," Stacy said, rubbing the wolf's head and sitting back down. She quickly read the rest of the words. *Quartz. Citrine. Copper. Amber. Garnet.* All gemstones. *Was the tundra explorer also a geologist? Was this just a list of the various rocks she'd uncovered in the different biomes she'd traveled to?*

Stacy walked over to her rocking chair and sat down. She wasn't sure what she had expected when she began her translations, but this certainly wasn't it. She'd hoped the rune would have contained some secret information about the wolves—something the tundra explorer couldn't risk writing down so that just anyone could find it and read it, but something important that needed to be recorded. Something someone like Stacy—a person who also knew the rune language and about the wolves' powers—would need to know. There had been no traces of gemstones in the glacier cavern and no mention of mining in the first entry of the journal Stacy had translated. *What am I missing?*

A week passed, and Pipsqueak continued to progress. For all his balking at having another animal in the cave, Everest had taken a real liking to Pipsqueak. Milquetoast loved Pipsqueak too and groomed him every day. He had finished his medicine and, just as Dr. Kay predicted, his appetite had returned. He could eat almost a whole salmon by himself now, which Stacy thought was a remarkable feat for a cat who was still so tiny.

Stacy hadn't looked at the rune since that first day back. She had set it aside and had been busying herself with chores around the cave. Since springtime was nearly in full swing, there was lot to accomplish. Stacy had worked for several days with Wink to chop wood to stack inside the cave, where it would stay dry. Spring was a strange season in the taiga. It could be sunny one hour and hailing the next. And there would inevitably be one or two surprise springtime snowstorms. Stacy wanted to have plenty of firewood to keep the cave warm.

The next day, however, was sunny, and Stacy decided it was a good day for a trip to the river. Noah would be able to fish for salmon there this time of year. Stacy wanted to dry a lot of fish skin to have around as treats for everyone. She and Addison had spent a lot of time over the past week drying the fish Noah had caught on their tundra expedition.

A trip to the river would also give Stacy the opportunity to wash all her winter clothes and store them for the season. And while they were there, she could forage for some wild asparagus. Sadly, it was too early in the year to find blackberries, Stacy's favorite. But if she found asparagus, perhaps she and Addison could attempt to make the breakfast Stacy had eaten at the diner. She'd been dreaming about it ever since.

Everest decided to stay with Pipsqueak and Milque-toast, along with Tucker, who was still sleeping more during the day than usual. And Addison had left the cave early to work the land over at the little grove where they farmed. Stacy suspected she wouldn't have wanted to go to the river anyway. *Addison hates it when her glasses get wet.*

This left Noah, Basil, Wink, Page, and Molly to accompany Stacy to the river. The six of them set off together. Basil wore a pack filled with Stacy's winter clothes. Stacy carried her satchel, as well as a folded-up piece of tarp to hold all the fish Noah would catch. It was the same tarp her wolves had used to carry Noah into the cave a few weeks ago when he'd been unconscious from a tranquilizer dart. He'd been able to sleep off the sedation in the cave, but boy, was Stacy grateful they'd had the tarp with them then.

The taiga was wet. Tiny droplets of dew were everywhere she looked on the way to the river, but Stacy knew the sun would soon dry everything up. A family of deer crossed in front of them, unfazed by Stacy and her clan, even Page and Molly. This made Stacy smile. She and her animals had truly become part of the forest. Stacy reached into her satchel and pulled out a handful of lingonberries to snack on while they walked.

The group reached the river and walked north along the shore for thirty minutes until they reached the waterfall where Stacy had once rescued a small rabbit with Everest and Noah. The waterfall was powerful during this time of year when all the snow from the mountains was melting. Stacy was grateful for the thundering noise from the falls—no one would be able to hear them as they splashed, barked, and yelled. The six of them spent an hour playing and soaking in the small hot springs Noah located on the west riverbank near the waterfall. Noah and Basil had a swimming competition to see who could swim the fastest while Stacy and Page treaded water, basking in the warmth of the water and the midday sun. Wink decided to climb to the top of the waterfall and jump several times, and Molly—poor Molly—sat on the shore of the river, determined not to get wet.

Eventually, Stacy and Page swam back across the river to where Molly was patiently waiting. Stacy spread out the tarp for Noah's fish and got to work washing her clothes while Page and Molly napped. Basil decided to help Noah with his fishing while Wink was off gallivanting somewhere. Stacy finished washing her clothes and laid them out to dry. She took the tundra explorer's journal and her own out from her satchel and began to translate another entry. When she was finished, she sat back and read it.

> *Spent the day with the male on the tundra, exercising his abilities, several of which have developed since I've come to live here. My current hypothesis is this new (or ancient?) species of wolves develop and deepen their powers throughout their lives. Whether they are born with them or they evolve, it is unclear, and I do not expect to know until our first litter of pups are born. His abilities are extraordinary—he can summon fire, freeze and unfreeze ice under his paws and, what is perhaps his strongest and oldest ability, he is able to show me past events by triggering memories in my mind—memories that are not even mine, but are his. I've taken to calling him Ames—short, of course, for Amethyst.*

Stacy stared at the last word of the journal entry. And then remembered the elder wolf's piercing purple eyes.

His name was Amethyst? Stacy flipped back to the rune she was trying to make sense of and then looked around at the wolves who had come to the river with her. Noah's blue eyes: lapis. Basil: citrine. Wink was back from his adventure, the now-setting sun glinting off his deep brown gaze: garnet. *It's their names!* Everest's eyes were silver like quartz, Tucker's were copper, and Addison's were amber. Stacy looked at the rune. It all made sense to her now. The rune was a perfect family tree. Stacy's wolves were the descendants of the tundra explorer's two wolves: Amethyst and Diamond. *Diamond. The wolf with prismatic eyes from the vision! Their mother!* And by that logic . . . there were two other wolves living in the mesa, Alpha and Beta, and . . . and four wolf pups! Stacy sat in stunned silence. *Diamond was crossed out in the ice cave and Ames was alone. I think that means she died. But there might be more magical wolves in the mesa? And maybe that's where the tundra explorer is too. We've got to go to the mesa!*

Stacy knew this wasn't the ideal time to take a trip away from the taiga, since Pipsqueak was only just regaining his strength, but the more she thought about the idea, the more she had to admit she liked it. Every other time she and her wolves had left the taiga, it had not been of their own volition. They were running away from guns: hunting rifles and tranquilizer darts. *This time will be different. This time it's on our terms. And Tucker will probably want to stay behind with the cats, which would be good since he still needs plenty of rest.*

Suddenly, Everest bounded into view, panting heavily as if he'd just sprinted from the cave to where Stacy was sitting on the bank of the river. *Oh, so you heard what I've been thinking about, have you, Everest? Well, let me have it. You probably think it's a terrible idea, right?* Stacy looked up from folding her clothes and into Everest's big gray eyes. She was surprised. *You . . . you want to go?* Stacy saw it right away in his expression. Longing. And Stacy understood completely. If there was even the smallest chance that she could find her family, she would jump at it. Her parents had died in a tragic accident—an accident she had survived. Stacy didn't like to think about it too much; she was happy with her life in the taiga after all. But she couldn't blame Everest for wanting to find more of his kind. And it had been her idea anyway!

"Everyone, gather round," Stacy said to the others who were still splashing around at the river's edge. "We're going back to the mesa!"

FIVE

STACY POURED A large handful of pumpkin seeds onto the top shelf of her bookcase, where Fluff roosted. A few days had passed since her epiphany about the possible existence of a mesa wolf pack. Stacy's group had been preparing to leave ever since.

Addison surprised Stacy by deciding to stay behind in the cave with Tucker and the cats. This made Stacy a little sad. After all, it had been Addison who led them across the tundra and deciphered the runes that led Stacy to theorize that there could *actually* be wolves in the mesa with similar powers. *We need Addi to come, don't we? I still can't read the runes without translating them first*. On the other hand, it did make Stacy feel better that someone was staying with Tucker as he continued to recover. Pipsqueak's recovery, however, had been nothing short of miraculous. The little guy was chasing Milquetoast around the cave practically nonstop at this point—pouncing on him and wrestling at all hours of the night (much to Everest's chagrin).

The cats were a handful now, but Addison would keep everything in order while the pack was away. She'd be able to continue all the spring planting in the garden and keep the cave tidy for when they returned. It was a good plan.

Stacy walked from the back of the cave to the center and placed the wolf backpack on Noah. She took her canteen and several gourds she had hollowed out over the winter and converted to water jugs, placing them in the pack.

"Sorry, this is going to be pretty heavy," she said to Noah as she tightened the strap around his chest. "Water was scarce in the mesa last time. We don't want to run out again. You and Everest can take turns carrying it."

Stacy walked over to the table where Addison had set out a huge spread of food for Stacy to pack in her satchel. There was dried fish, dried apples and berries, pumpkin bread, boiled eggs, Brussels sprouts, turnips, pine needles for Stacy to brew tea with, and a small pile of birch bark (for Stacy to chew on if food was low and she got desperate). And at the end of the table was an almost-empty jar of peanut butter—the jar Stacy had bought when she had been in the mesa and had gone to a grocery store for the first time.

"The last of the peanut butter, Addi?" Stacy said with reverence. "Are you sure?"

Addison nodded, and Stacy threw her arms around the wolf. Not because of the peanut butter gift, but because she would miss Addison and the others so much. Still, Stacy was excited to learn more about the wolves' ancestry . . . and maybe even find the author of the journal herself. Another element that made Stacy feel slightly better about leaving was that she knew, with it being rainy season in the taiga, that they'd be trapped in the cave for most of the month if they stayed in the forest. *This will be a fun adventure.* And Stacy was certain there would be some thrilling animal rescues along the way.

"Come here, Milquetoast!" Stacy said, calling softly to the cat, who made a small meow and walked over to her. Stacy picked him up, cradling him in her arms and kissing the top of his head. "I'm sorry I keep leaving you. Just wait until our first winter together—it's going to be nothing but scratches behind the ears while I read books in the rocking chair with you on my lap, I promise."

Stacy set the tiny white cat down and watched as he scampered over to his favorite spot in front of the fire. Pipsqueak was in the back of the cave, playing with the small water stream where Stacy sometimes kept the fish Noah killed until Addison had time to cook them for her. Stacy reached into her pocket and pulled out a small piece of dried fish skin. She broke it in half and offered one of the pieces to Milquetoast, then walked to the back of the cave where Pipsqueak was.

"Here you go, Pip," Stacy said, placing the treat down at the kitten's paws. "Be good for Addison and Tucker. Keep eating, and I'll see you soon."

Stacy wasn't sure how long they'd be gone, but she couldn't imagine it being more than a fortnight.

"What's the plan, Everest?" Stacy said, turning toward the large wolf, who was standing near the map of the taiga Stacy had drawn with chalk on one of the cave walls. "Should we catch a ride on the freight train again?"

Everest shook his head.

"You want to *run* the whole way?" Stacy asked, a hint of incredulity in her tone.

Basil ran up to them and spun in circles. Wink joined her. Stacy looked at them both. *Basil is the fastest wolf, no question. But if I had to rank the others, Addison and Tucker would probably be the slowest of the pack. With them staying behind, Everest, Wink, and Noah could probably keep up with Basil pretty well. And I suppose Page and Molly could ride on Wink while I ride on Basil—I have another saddlebag that I could put Page and Molly in the pockets of, on either side of Wink's back. . . .*

"All right," she said. "Let's go for it."

The group set out, heading south, and ran for a very long time—hours—stopping only occasionally for the wolves to lap up water from streams they found along the way. They ran well into the evening, chasing the sunset until the darkness caught up with them. Basil led the way in the dark with Stacy on her back, followed by Wink, with Page and Molly on his back, Noah and Everest at the rear. They were still running as Stacy began to nod off for the night. She tied her wrists together with a magenta bandanna she had and looped her arms around Basil's neck. She wouldn't get good rest tonight—it was like being half asleep, stirring every time Basil jumped or changed direction suddenly—but Stacy knew she would catch up on sleep when they reached the mesa, and night was a safe time for the wolves to be traveling.

Stacy woke to the smell of trout cooking over coals. They must have stopped running at some point during the night, but Stacy hadn't woken up. She was curled up against Wink; Page and Molly were at her feet. Noah was turning the fish over with a stick, and Basil stoked the coals with her nose. Stacy looked around for Everest and found him sitting on a rock ten feet above her, keeping lookout. The sun must have just come up—it was light enough to see, but just barely. Stacy strained her eyes to take in the landscape around her. *Wait, that can't be right, can it?* Everywhere she looked were . . . flowers. Tulips of every color—white, orange, pink, red—blush pink peonies, red rose bushes, white-and-yellow oxeye daisies, and blue cornflowers dotted the hilly terrain. Stacy stood up in excitement, the sun now peeking through the tall oak trees that surrounded them. Bees flew through the air, buzzing around Stacy.

"A flower . . . forest?" Stacy said in awe.

She spun around in a circle, taking in all the beautiful blooms around her. She was suddenly filled with gratitude for Everest's idea to run to the mesa. *We definitely didn't see this from the train.* Wink ran over to her, a freshly picked daisy in his mouth, and tucked the flower in Stacy's hair.

"Thank you, Wink," she said.

Suddenly, Page started barking loudly. Stacy spun around to see what she was barking at. *A beehive!*

Hanging on a large oak tree was a round beehive, buzzing with bees.

"Page, get back!" Stacy commanded. "They're the reason this forest is filled with flowers. Let them do their work."

The group ate breakfast and basked in their beautiful surroundings for a bit before pressing on to the mesa. Stacy had a lot of time to think while she rode on Basil's back. *What a crazy thing I've done. I've brought four of my wolves and both of my dogs out of hiding and on a quest to find other wolves who . . . should also be in hiding. Where do we even begin looking for them anyway?*

Stacy reassured herself that it would be okay. Even if they didn't find the other wolves, everyone loved the mesa biome, and it would be a fun vacation of sorts while the taiga was still a bit cold and rainy. Secretly though, Stacy hoped they would find more of her wolves' kind. And she knew Everest felt the same.

Hours passed as the pack ran through different biomes: the flower forest, a hilly birch forest, a swamp, plains, sunflower fields . . . and then, way out in the distance, Stacy glimpsed the first red cliff of the mesa biome.

"Up there!" she called out. "There's the mesa!"

Basil looked up and zagged in the direction Stacy had

pointed. Stacy looked behind her at the others. Page and Molly were clinging on for dear life as Wink bounded along. Noah looked calm; his gait was fluid and swift like a river. Everest was in the back still, his head about a foot above the others. He gave Stacy a confident look and continued to run at a steady pace.

Stacy looked down and saw the ground beneath Basil's paws change from dirt to red sand. *The mesa.* It felt a bit like coming home to Stacy, which confused her, since she'd lived in the taiga all her life. She took in the now familiar smells of sage and cactus flower that perfumed the wind in the mesa.

"Basil." Stacy leaned down and whispered in the wolf's ear. "Let's cut to the west and make camp in the abandoned mineshaft we stayed in last time."

Basil nodded and immediately changed the group's direction. Stacy glanced backward and got a nod of approval from Everest. *I still have no idea what we're doing down here, but at least we'll be somewhere familiar.*

The seven of them traversed the rocky scree at the bottom of the mesa where the abandoned mineshaft was located. Stacy was eager to reach their destination and stretch her legs, but she was grateful to still be on Basil's back as the wolf nimbly navigated through the cactus and tumbleweeds that dotted the trail up to the mine-shaft entrance.

The mineshaft was exactly as Stacy had remembered it. Cool. Damp. Protected. *We'll be safe here.* Stacy set about making the mineshaft's entrance hospitable for the group. First, she stacked as many tumbleweeds as she could find up against the large timbers at the mineshaft's opening to create a makeshift doorway. She spread out the tarp she'd brought (which she had cleaned since Noah used it to carry fish) on the ground toward the back of the entrance. *We'll sleep here. That way, if someone finds us, we can escape by running down the mineshaft's tunnels and hiding.* She put the few pieces of extra clothing she'd brought—her flannel shirt and her navy sweater—down on top of the tarp. *Page and Molly can nap here during the day.* Next, she and Basil made a small firepit near the entrance. Stacy gathered pieces of kindling and deadwood and stacked them beside the firepit. And then she set out the food Addison had packed for them. *This looks like it would last us about a week at most. We'll need to scavenge more if we want to stay here any longer than that.*

Stacy spent the rest of the afternoon sketching a map of the mesa in her notebook, including the landmarks she could remember from the last time they'd visited. She wanted to have the lay of the land for when they began exploring. Sunset came, and Stacy watched it with the others, high up on the mesa. The sky turned purple and pink and finally gray before night settled over their home away from home.

Stacy slept soundly the first night in the mesa, nuzzled alongside Basil, Wink, and Noah with Page and Molly, while Everest slept with one eye open near the mineshaft entrance.

Sunshine poked its way through the tumbleweeds and the two wooden pillars that formed the entrance to the mine. It woke Stacy gently. She got up and stretched and then walked over to the fire Basil had made and brewed some pine needle tea to drink along with some of Addison's pumpkin bread, warmed up and toasted.

Stacy walked outside the mineshaft, still chewing her last bite of pumpkin bread, and took a deep breath. Tilting her head upward, she was amazed by how big the blue sky was. She never had this wide of a view back in the taiga, with its towering spruce trees. Stacy was still gazing up at the sky when she noticed several vultures circling not too far in the distance.

"We should go there," Stacy said to Everest, pointing

up at the vultures. "I hate to say it, but there is probably a dead animal there. You'd be able to scare off any coyotes and eat." *I know it's gross to eat a decomposing animal— well, to me at least—but if the animal has already passed away, at least it would be providing sustenance and energy to another animal with its death.*

Everest nodded solemnly. Stacy turned to the others.

"Noah, how about you stay here with Page and Molly," Stacy said. She wanted one of the wolves to stay with the dogs, but she also knew that he would prefer to eat the fish they'd brought anyway.

Everest, Basil, Wink, and Stacy set out from the mineshaft and across the mesa toward where the vultures were flying in slow and droopy circles. Stacy steeled herself for the potentially grisly scene they were about to encounter. Basil led them down a steep ravine and into a thicket of low shrubs. Quail, jackrabbits, and lizards scurried out of their way. Basil slowed down, and the four of them crept closer and closer to the spot where the vultures were directly overhead. They were mere feet away now. Basil and Everest each took branches from the bushes in their mouths, peeling them back to reveal a small clearing. Stacy gasped in horror.

There, in the middle of the clearing in the desert, lay a lone wolf so skeleton-like that Stacy could see the shapes of each and every one of his bones sticking out through his pale white fur.

SIX

STACY STARED AT the skeleton wolf intently. Suddenly, his bony rib cage lifted and fell—a breath! *He's alive, Everest!* But only barely. Stacy's mind raced. *Everest, you and I can probably manage to lift him onto Basil's or Wink's back—probably Basil since she's fastest—who can carry the wolf back to the mineshaft. We can save him if we move quickly.*

Stacy took a cautious step toward the wolf. Suddenly, his head jerked up and his eyes opened. He stared directly at Stacy with the blackest eyes she'd ever seen and then bared his teeth and growled. Stacy took a step backward and held up her hands as Everest stepped forward, ducking under one of her arms to wrap himself protectively around her body, snarling back at the defenseless wolf. Just then, without warning, a second wolf emerged from the bushes. This wolf was also white, except for her paws, which were stained a reddish-brown color, as if from digging in the mesa's terracotta clay. She had little bits of twigs and sage sticking out from her ratty fur—Stacy even spotted a tiny yellow cactus flower and a few needles near her neck.

The wolf quickly ran to her skeletal pack member and laid some type of food in front of him. Stacy focused her eyes to see what it was, but the wolf quickly ate the offering and jumped to his feet. Before Stacy could react at all, the wolf with all the sticks sticking out of her and the skeleton wolf sprinted off away from Stacy and her wolves.

"Follow them!" Stacy yelled. "They must be the wolves we came to find!" Everest and Wink were already in pursuit. Stacy looked around and saw Basil, crouching low to the ground. Stacy hopped on Basil's back and held tightly as Basil rocketed off toward the others.

Basil quickly passed Wink and Everest, who had both gained some ground on the two wolves. They climbed quickly out of the ravine and were running across the

mesa, dodging and weaving through the mesa biome's huge red boulders that had fallen from the cliffs above them, perhaps centuries ago. The wolf with the little bits of sticks and brush sticking out of her fur glanced back at Stacy and Basil as she ran. Suddenly, Basil veered to the right to avoid a large tumbleweed. Stacy tightened her grip on Basil's fur and braced herself as six or seven tumbleweeds came rolling at them like a set of waves. Basil slowed and navigated around them with ease and then quickly sped up to close the distance she'd lost. The disheveled wolf glanced back at Basil. Suddenly, as if out of thin air, a giant thicket of sagebrush grew up out of the red sand—too wide to run around and higher than Basil could jump. Stacy's head was spinning, but out of the corner of her eye she saw Everest catching up to her and Basil. He passed them, running faster than Stacy had ever seen him run, and skidded to a halt right in front of the wall of sagebrush. Red sand flew up as Everest's sturdy paws dug deep into the earth to halt his momentum. Basil accelerated, and in one smooth motion, she jumped on Everest's back and propelled herself and Stacy into the air and onto the other side of the barrier. Stacy turned around to see Wink soaring over the wall after them, landing with a massive thud on the soft sand. Everest would have to go around, but with Basil and Wink on the other side now, the chase continued.

The skeleton wolf was slowing down a bit now, struggling to keep up with the other wolf, who glanced over her shoulder again—this time her eyes were wide with panic. She slowed down a bit to cross a dry arroyo and Stacy could feel Basil speed up to finally overtake her and the skeleton wolf.

But suddenly, a prickly pear cactus no bigger than one of Stacy's boots doubled in size the second the two mesa wolves passed it. It doubled again and again and too many times to count as Basil sprinted toward it. Huge needles stuck out in every direction and Stacy braced herself for the worst while Basil skidded in the sand, trying to stop, but she was going too fast. Just before Basil and Stacy crashed into them, Wink charged by, barreling through the cactus—his power allowing him to emerge on the other side completely unscathed. Seeing the pathway cleared, Basil jerked forward, resuming the chase. Within a minute, Basil and Wink had caught up to the two mesa wolves and were running on either side of them. The skeleton wolf looked exhausted. Stacy looked at the female mesa wolf. Her expression looked to Stacy as if she were out of ideas and resigned to being caught. *She* is *doing this,* Stacy realized. *She has a power!*

Stacy heard a bark behind her and whipped her head around. *Everest!* He'd caught up to them and was only a few paces behind. Basil surged one last time to overtake the mesa wolves. She spun around, stopping them in their tracks. Wink went to the side and turned to face the mesa wolves as well, forming a triangle with himself, Basil, and Everest. There was nowhere for the wolves to run, and by the looks of the skeleton wolf, who had slumped down at the feet of the other, he was done running.

Stacy hopped off Basil's back and broke a branch off a nearby dead bush and quickly scrawled the rune symbols for *friend* in the red dirt. The wolves' expressions remained unchanged.

"Well, it was worth a try," Stacy said glumly.

Basil quickly stepped forward and touched her nose to the dead bush Stacy had broken the branch from, incinerating it instantly. This got the mesa wolves' attention. The female stepped forward to Basil and walked in a circle around the ashes of the dead bush, her bushy tail gently waving in the desert wind. She took a step back, and Stacy gasped. The bush had reappeared and was no longer dead. Stacy walked forward to examine it.

"It's real!" she exclaimed. "She used her power!"

Wink and Basil walked toward the skeleton wolf and

gently lifted him up and laid him over Everest's broad back. The female wolf began to lead Everest and the others up the steep terrain of the mesa. *Everest, can we trust them?* Stacy thought to herself as she walked alongside her pack's alpha. Everest turned to her and nodded, reassuring Stacy.

Stacy was in disbelief for much of their journey up to the top of the mesa. *The rune was right. There are other wolves here with powers.* Stacy already had a guess as to what the female mesa wolf's power was, but it was strange. *She appears to be able to make things grow . . . like some type of bonemeal effect. Could be useful. But it sure is peculiar.* What the skeleton wolf's power might be, Stacy had no idea.

The group was now high on the mesa, above the hoodoos that rose in the distance, above the abandoned mineshaft where Noah, Page, and Molly were hiding out. They were almost as high up as the clouds. The female wolf led them to a cluster of cacti, which she parted using her powers to reveal a small gully in the earth a few feet below the mesa's surface. There was a patch of soft-looking grass, a shallow pond, and . . . Stacy blinked . . . two more wolves!

SEVEN

EVEREST STEPPED DOWN into the gully and laid
the skeleton wolf down on the grass. One by one, the
rest of the group followed Everest below the ground as
the cactus filled in above them. Wink and Basil stayed
near the entrance . . . what was left of it. Stacy noticed
her wolves seemed a little uneasy and then realized what
the reason must be. *We're outnumbered. Four wolves to
three.* Stacy walked back to Wink and Basil and put a
hand on each of them and whispered to them.

"These wolves are special, just like you both," Stacy
said. "It's going to be okay."

Stacy turned and walked over and knelt by the

skeleton wolf. She ran her hand down his lean frame.

"Ribsy," Stacy said softly. "That's what I'm going to call you. Here, have something to eat."

. Stacy reached into her satchel and pulled out her jar of peanut butter. She knew the treat would be rich in protein and fat and would be good for the gaunt wolf. The wolf eagerly ate the peanut butter, and Stacy watched in amazement as Ribsy's rib cage swelled and filled out. His bones were no longer visible. He licked the jar clean and laid his head down to rest. The female wolf came over and nuzzled Stacy's shoulder, grateful for her help.

"Of course, girl," Stacy said, taking the wolf's head in both her hands and rubbing her ears for a proper introduction. "It's nice to meet you."

Stacy plucked the cactus flower that was stuck to the wolf's neck and tucked it into the thick fur around the wolf's ear. Next, Stacy carefully removed the sharp needles buried in the wolf's pelt next to where the flower had been. A small drop of bright red blood appeared where Stacy pulled out the biggest needle. She quickly untied the bandanna around her collar and wrapped it around the wolf's neck, then sat back to admire how pretty the green-eyed wolf was with the purple cactus flower and the magenta bandanna. Stacy looked at the bandanna's intricate paisley pattern.

"Paisley," Stacy said. "I think that name suits you."

Paisley licked Stacy's face, and the whole mood of the underground chamber seemed to lighten. Basil and Wink appeared less tense. And Stacy turned her attention to the other two wolves, completely unprepared for what she was about to see.

The other two wolves had been cowering in the corner of the underground space. A male and a female. The male wolf almost looked like a ghost. But not in the sense that he was wasting away, like Ribsy had been when Stacy first encountered him. No, this wolf appeared healthy and large . . . but had silver fur that was so fluffy and fine that it was almost translucent. Stacy stared at him, transfixed. The wolf's fur reminded her of the baby goslings she had seen last spring at the river with Noah. Their fuzzy down had been so soft and airy. Stacy had described them in her journal as feeling like what she imagined it would be to touch a wispy cloud. His eyes were bright blue, like the sky on a particularly sunny day. They stared back at Stacy intensely.

Stacy turned to study the female next to him. Her hind legs were sat down, submerged in the shallow pond, while her front half was sitting up, elegant and poised, but subdued and still . . . statuesque even. She got up from the water and walked over to Stacy to greet her.

Out of the water, her fur hardened into place. Stacy ran her fingers down the wolf's back. Her coat was stiff and so brittle that Stacy hoped she wasn't in any pain. But she was. The wolf winced a little at Stacy's soft touch. Ribsy ran over to the wolf, pressing his body against hers. Her fur softened a bit and Ribsy grew leaner. He helped her back over to the pond and into the water and then collapsed, looking weary and skeletal again. *I don't know what is going on here, but it's not good,* Stacy thought to herself so Everest could hear her. *I thought it was only Ribsy who was in bad shape, but this female wolf seems even worse. This pack definitely isn't thriving here in the mesa . . . in fact, they seem to be barely surviving.* Everest nodded glumly. Stacy was unsure what her next step should be. She was suddenly filled with remorse that the two wolves who had stayed behind in the taiga were exactly the two wolves whose powers might have been of use to the mesa wolf pack. Tucker, if he himself was healed, could fix whatever seemed to be ailing the female wolf in the water. And Stacy would love to consult with Addison about what she thought was happening with Ribsy. *Perhaps the tundra explorer's journal mentions this pack in the pages I haven't translated?*

Stacy sat down and flipped to a random page in the middle of the journal. *Here goes nothing.* She began quickly translating one sentence at a time until she had decoded an entire diary entry. She hastily read through it, scanning for any mention of the mesa wolves.

Time flies! I can scarcely believe we've made five visits to the tundra already this year. When we moved away from the tundra seven years ago when I became pregnant, we'd given up hope completely that Ames and Diamond would ever produce pups. Imagine our surprise when we discovered Diamond was pregnant on our routine trip to the tundra this year. We've been visiting as often as possible making preparations for the birthing and today was the big day. Diamond birthed five pups beginning at 05:19 this morning. Three males and two females. We won't know what color eyes they have for a week or two, but all appear to be strong and healthy. We've only been back in the tundra about a week, but plan to stay here for the next several weeks to monitor the pups' progress. Ames has made remarkable improvements to our crude glacier home in the years we've been away—I daresay it's almost palatial now with all the spacious additions he's created.

Stacy stopped reading. She didn't know what to do. She'd obviously picked the wrong entry, and every moment she spent translating the explorer's journal was precious time they were wasting not helping these wolves. The explorer's entry was interesting, but it provided no help to Stacy's current situation.

If Addison were here, then she could read ahead. It would take me hours, if not days, to translate enough of it to find something. Stacy looked over to Ribsy and the female wolf who was now slumped next to Paisley; both wolves had sorrowful expressions. They didn't have time for Stacy to translate the journal.

Stacy wasn't sure exactly what she should do, but she knew that they all couldn't stay in the small ditch in the mesa. *We can't take them all the way back to the taiga, Everest. I doubt they'd survive the journey. But let's at least get them to the mineshaft and make them a decent meal. From there we can decide what to do next.* Everest nodded in agreement and walked over to the large cloud-like wolf. There was a tense exchange between them, and for a moment, Stacy wondered if the mesa pack wouldn't want to come with them. *I can't blame them. They just met us. And who even knows if they've interacted with a human before. Maybe they never met the tundra explorer. . . .*

Stacy looked around at each pair of the wolves' sad eyes: blue . . . black . . . green . . . aqua. *Wait! The tundra explorer referred to them just as numbers in the rune. She never saw them up close. Everest, you need to explain to him who we are!*

Everest continued to stare at the large wispy wolf. The wolf nodded occasionally, taking in everything Everest was showing him in his mind, just as Ames had done with Everest and Stacy in the tundra. After a while, Everest turned to Stacy and gave her a nod. They were ready to leave together.

Stacy looked up at the green-and-purple cacti canopy covering them—the sky had turned the same shade as the purple cactus. Twilight. It would be a difficult journey back to the mineshaft with the two weakened wolves and an exhausted Paisley. But Stacy was determined to save this pack.

"All right everyone," Stacy said, standing up. "Let's get going. If we're lucky we can make it to the mineshaft before nightfall."

EIGHT

THE FULL MOON was high in the sky as Stacy, Everest, Basil, and Wink filed into the abandoned mineshaft. They were greeted enthusiastically by Page, Molly, and Noah, who all ran around in excited circles, barking and wagging their tails until they suddenly realized the presence of the others. Ribsy, Paisley, and the other two wolves walked slowly through the mineshaft's entrance. Ribsy and the female wolf were walking slowly, as they were clearly weak and unwell. Paisley and the male mesa wolf walked slowly because they were apprehensive of entering a new place and meeting Stacy's dogs.

Eventually, everyone greeted one another and settled

down for the evening. Basil made a fire, and Stacy prepared as much food as she could for the group. Their meal consisted of all of the fish Noah had brought from the mesa, filleted and fried, along with roasted Brussels sprouts and turnips from Addison's garden, and some cactus pear that Noah had foraged while they were gone and Basil had charred over the coals of the fire.

There was barely enough food for everyone. Stacy was positive each wolf could have eaten at least triple the portion she doled out, but the new wolves seemed grateful, and everyone finished their meals . . . even the Brussels sprouts.

The meal, meager as it was, seemed to revive Ribsy. He looked back to normal. Paisley was napping peacefully next to the wolf Stacy thought looked like a giant puffy cloud. She'd spent the entire trek from the mesa wolves' den to the mineshaft trying to come up with a good name for him. Something that reminded Stacy of the sky, clouds, or heavens. She would have named him Celeste, but he didn't look like a Celeste. She thought about simply calling him Cloud, but his aura was not soft enough to convincingly carry off the name Cloud. For as delicate and flimsy as his exterior seemed, his personality was anything but. He was commanding, and a bit austere, and Stacy even wondered if he was the mesa pack's alpha. She'd finally settled on the name Atlas. *Celestial. Strong. A name fit for a leader.*

As for the last wolf in the mesa pack—the one who had been in the water when Stacy first found her—Stacy had been trying out the name Pearl for her, as her coat was not as brilliant white as her own wolves' but had a type of mother-of-pearl iridescence to it. The name was a good one, but Stacy was more concerned that Pearl had not perked up since arriving at the abandoned mineshaft. She'd managed to choke down her dinner, but the food had not done anything to improve her coat, which was crusty and cracking. Noah kept making trips down the mineshaft to water springs and carrying back a bucketful in one of the gourds they'd brought, so he could dump the water on her to temporarily soften her hard, brittle coat before heading back down the mine for more water.

Stacy was exhausted from the events of the day, but her mind was racing as everyone bedded down for the night. *Why didn't we encounter the mesa pack the first time we visited the mesa? Did the mesa pack hide from us? How much longer can Pearl survive like this? Does she have a power? Is she dying? Does Atlas have a power? What is it? What should I do if Pearl isn't better in the morning? What would Addison do?* Stacy tossed and turned all night against Wink and Basil.

In the morning, Pearl was alive, but only barely. Noah was weary from staying up all night attending to her. It seemed as though he had taken an instant liking to her. Judging by the fact that Everest and Atlas were still fast asleep, Stacy surmised that Noah must have enlisted their help during the night to push an enormous iron mine cart up from the mines. *How on earth did they get this up here? And how tired was I that the sound didn't wake me up?* Noah must have filled the mine cart with water, because Pearl was currently soaking in it. Stacy walked over to Pearl, who looked sullen. Stacy reached into her satchel and pulled out some dried fish. Pearl instantly lifted her head and cocked it to one side. Stacy fed her the dried fish and watched as Pearl transformed. Her hair was now silken and flowing and her back legs and tail moved gracefully in the small amount of water in the mine cart. Noah woke up and walked over, his eyes wide. Clearly, Pearl had not looked like this all night while Stacy was asleep. Pearl dipped under the water and then reemerged, sticking just her head and snout over the top of the mine cart. Noah came nose-to-nose with Pearl, and then suddenly, Pearl lifted her snout and spat a bit of the water out like a fountain onto Noah's face and then quickly disappeared under the water again.

Stacy laughed as Noah shook his head and peered down over the edge into the mine cart where Pearl was turning circles.

Everest got up and walked over to where Stacy and Noah were standing and looked at Pearl and then to Stacy with a quizzical expression. *I don't know, Ever. She just . . . perked up all of a sudden.* Stacy was relieved Pearl was feeling better. It was as if a huge weight was lifted from everyone in the mineshaft for a few hours that morning. Stacy decided to decode more of the tundra explorer's journal to see if she would learn where the explorer had gone when she'd left the tundra. *It must have been to the mesa, right? Hopefully I can learn something—anything—that will help Pearl.*

The wolf pups have all opened their eyes and are doing well. Quartz is the biggest by far. He eats the most and I'm confident he'll become the largest of the litter. Personality traits are calm, quiet, and observant. Copper is quite large as well, although most of it is fluff. He loves to snuggle. Lapis and Citrine are well matched as playmates, with Citrine usually able to get the best of him. She is

remarkably agile for her age. Amber was
the last of the litter to open her eyes, but
that seems to have worked to her advantage.
Her senses are superior to the others': smell,
hearing, balance. She may be the smartest,
although only time will tell.

Stacy looked out of the mineshaft at the afternoon sun. She hadn't realized how much time she had spent poring over the explorer's diary. She could read about her wolf pack as pups forever. It was fascinating, and Stacy wished more than anything that she could make faster progress in translating the journal's pages so she could see if there was anything in it that would help Pearl. But it was getting late in the day now, and only Page and Molly had remained with her, tucked away in the back of the mineshaft entrance. Stacy stood up to check on what the wolves had gotten up to while she was engrossed in the journal.

The only wolves who were still in the mineshaft were Noah and Pearl. Stacy walked over to them, eager to spend more time getting to know Pearl—but she stopped short when she was a few feet from the mine cart. Pearl was slumped over and sleeping. *She's not feeling well again*. Stacy put her arm around Noah's giant body.

"We'll figure out a way to get her better, don't worry."

Atlas was near as well, watching over Pearl. Stacy wished more than anything she could communicate with these wolves the way she could with her own. It would happen in time, she was sure—*if we have a lot more time together, that is.* Stacy was amazed that the mesa pack had been able to keep Pearl alive this whole time by themselves. Clearly it had taken a toll on Ribsy's health. And left Paisley constantly frazzled. And made Atlas standoffish and stressed. *It must have been so hard for them.*

Stacy turned toward the entrance of the mineshaft and saw that Basil had made a large fire. Next to the fire sat Ribsy, with several dead jackrabbits and a small javelina nearby.

"Basil!" Stacy exclaimed. "What . . . what happened here?"

Stacy realized what must have happened before she had finished her sentence. The mesa wolves obviously didn't follow the same unusual diet her taiga pack adhered to around Stacy. They would of course hunt here—not only was there not much to eat in the desert, but they didn't appear to have a human companion like Stacy around who would have encouraged them to eat more . . . civilized meals. Pearl was probably a good fisher like Noah, but not in her current condition or without a nearby river or lake. So this must be what they ate. Stacy looked at the grisly scene, but then remembered that even her wolves used to eat chickens they raised for slaughter. Stacy shuddered at the memory of it.

"Um . . . well done, Ribsy," Stacy said in an unconvincing tone. She wasn't thrilled at the sight of the dead animals, but she had to remind herself that it was a good thing that both the mesa pack and her own would eat well tonight.

She left Basil and Ribsy to their meal preparation and walked farther out onto the mesa. There was something in the distance that Stacy couldn't quite make out. It looked like Everest and Paisley were busying themselves around . . . *Are they bushes . . . ? Or . . . ?* Stacy took a few quick steps forward. She couldn't believe it. They were crops!

Stacy ran down the hill to where Paisley and Everest were standing. There was a small but very well-organized garden that had definitely not been there that morning. There were a few rows of beetroot, carrots, and what looked to be corn—although it would be months before the corn grew tall enough to pick and eat. But just as Stacy had finished taking in the scene, Paisley began walking around each crop in a tight circle. *Of course! Her bonemeal effect!* Everest was watching her intently as well. The crops grew instantly. Paisley plucked an ear of corn from the stalk with her mouth and threw it to Everest, who caught it and brought it over to Stacy. Stacy held the corn in her hands, peeling back its layers to reveal bright golden yellow kernels.

"Incredible," Stacy said. "I'll roast this over Basil's fire!"

Stacy, the taiga pack, the mesa pack, Page, and Molly stuffed themselves. Well . . . everyone except for Pearl. None of the food appealed to her. She poked around at some of the fish and then retired back to the mine cart. Stacy had eaten her fill of corn on the cob and had no desire whatsoever to watch as the wolves gnawed on javelina or jackrabbit, so she went to the back of the mineshaft to update her journal. Now more than ever, it was important to her to keep her own record of her interactions with the wolves—both her own and the mystic mesa pack. She had been inspired by the author of the journal and hoped that one day they would meet. *I bet she would know how to help Pearl.*

Stacy finished writing in her journal by candlelight— candles she'd crafted with Addison and that Basil lit for her with her nose. Stacy tucked her journal into her satchel for safekeeping, wedging it between the tundra explorer's journal, the flint and steel Basil had given her as a gift last fall, her climbing rope, and the few pieces of dried fish that were left. Stacy held the package of dried fish and a thought crept slowly across her mind. *This is what helped Pearl feel better earlier today . . . even if for just a short while . . . this is something.* Stacy couldn't wait to test her theory. She walked over to the mine cart Pearl was soaking in and waved a piece of dried fish in front of her nose. The reaction was instantaneous. Pearl bit down on the fish and opened her eyes at the same moment. Stacy gave her all of it, even allowing Pearl to nose around the scrap of fabric for the crumbly bits of fish skin. Pearl experienced a similar transformation to the one she'd had earlier that day—her coat seemed smoother and her spirits were bolstered.

Stacy returned to the back of the cave where she slept with Page and Molly and her wolves. Everyone was in the process of settling down to sleep. *Pearl obviously needs to eat fish. Noah prefers fish, but it's like she* has *to have it to thrive. But how has she survived this long in the desert without it? And why didn't she feel better after eating the fish we prepared for her the first night we brought her back to the mineshaft? What was different between the fish then and my dried fish?*

The answer came to Stacy like a bolt of lightning coming down from a storm cloud, and it knocked the breath right out of her.

"Oh!" she gasped. "I . . . oh, oh . . . Everest!"

The alpha wolf stirred from his position at the mineshaft's entrance—Stacy could just make out his face glowing in the light of the moon.

The fish we gave Pearl the first night we met her were the ones Noah caught in the taiga before we left. They were river salmon.

Everest looked at Stacy with a perplexed expression as Stacy continued in excited thought, now standing and pacing anxiously back and forth in the mineshaft.

The salmon Addison and I dried . . . the salmon that I gave Pearl this morning and just now . . . the only thing we've tried that has made her feel better . . . is not from the taiga. It was from the tundra. It's not river salmon. It's Arctic salmon. Pearl needs salt. Pearl needs . . . the ocean!

NINE

STACY COULDN'T BELIEVE she'd figured it out. And she'd worked it out without Addison's help . . . or help from the tundra explorer's journal. Stacy did it on her own. *Maybe I actually am smart for my age. Maybe I really could go to school like Miriam said. . . .* Of course, it was just a theory at this point. Stacy wouldn't know for sure that Pearl needed salt water unless they brought her to the ocean and tested it out. But even that wouldn't explain why she was sick now. *Could Pearl have been born near the ocean?* Stacy was pretty sure Pearl was one of the four wolf pups listed on the tundra explorer's rune.

It didn't make any sense. *Unless . . . what if her powers only recently developed? Just like my wolves—this is new for them. One of my wolves could have developed a power that was dependent on a biome too. We're just lucky that didn't happen.*

Stacy looked over to Everest—his face bore a pensive expression, like he was slowly taking in the surge of Stacy's thoughts and considering each one of them carefully. The reality was that Stacy and her pack had no other ideas about how to help Pearl. And it seemed like Pearl was running out of time. They could either stay here and watch Pearl continue to suffer, or they could take a leap of faith and test Stacy's hypothesis.

"Where is the nearest ocean?" Stacy wondered aloud, walking over to Everest. She'd been to the ocean once when she was young—probably eight or nine years old—she'd gone with her pack but could barely remember the trip. And that must have been near the taiga, farther north than where they were now in the mesa. Suddenly, Atlas came to Stacy's side. Stacy felt a cool breeze move through her hair and took a deep breath of it. Atlas pointed his nose in a direction—southeast.

"Knew I was right to name you Atlas," Stacy said. She wanted to pat him on the head, but she wasn't sure Atlas would enjoy that. She still wasn't sure where she stood with the mesa pack's leader. "How far?"

Everest confabbed with Atlas and walked over to the firepit. He took three stones and laid them at Stacy's feet.

"Three days?" Stacy asked. Everest nodded.

Three days. How does Atlas know that? Has he been there before? Has Pearl been there before? Can she survive three more days? What if we bring her all the way there away from her home and that's not even what she needs?

Stacy's plan was risky. But one look at Pearl was all Stacy needed to find the resolve to head east to the ocean. *Everest, please do your best to explain to Atlas, Ribsy, and Paisley why we should go. I'll go tell the others.*

Stacy walked over to where Basil, Wink, and Noah were standing next to Pearl in the mine cart. Stacy gently placed her hand on Pearl's head. The wolf barely stirred.

"We're going to try to make you better," she said, and then looked toward the others. "Everest and I think taking Pearl to the ocean where she can swim freely is the best chance to get her strength back." The wolves nodded in understanding. Stacy ran her hand down the back of Pearl's head and neck; the wolf's fur was dry and crackly. *Hang in there, girl.*

Ribsy walked over to them and touched his nose to Pearl's. The effect was immediate. Stacy could almost see the transfer of energy that took place before her. As Ribsy grew weaker and thinner, new life was breathed into Pearl—her chest expanded, her coat softened, and her beautiful turquoise eyes opened and looked appreciatively at Ribsy, who was now skin and bones again. *That settles it. Ribsy is a healer just like Tucker. Although it weakens him so much . . . It's almost like he's taking some of his life and giving it to whoever he's healing.*

"Quick," Stacy said to Wink and Basil. "Help him over to the fire and get him something to eat."

Basil and Wink helped Ribsy to lie down by the fire. Noah brought him water to drink, and Basil brought him a piece of javelina jerky from the batch she was drying. Ribsy ate and drank eagerly and then fell asleep. *Good. He needs to rest up for the journey.*

Stacy spent the rest of the morning packing up the mineshaft and playing with Page and Molly (who were sure to become incredibly bored on a three-day journey to the beach). As she carried the last of her belongings to the front of the mineshaft, a thought occurred to her. *We should carve runes on the mineshaft walls—just like in the glacier cavern on the tundra!* Stacy couldn't believe she hadn't thought of it before. What if the tundra explorer came looking for them and found this place? There would be no record of the mesa wolves ever being here. Stacy used her pickaxe to chip her rune message into the stone. She included each member of the mesa pack, assigning gemstone names to them. Topaz for Atlas, Emerald for Paisley, Obsidian for Ribsy, and Aquamarine for Pearl. Stacy carved Pearl's gemstone name faintly into the stone, to indicate that she was weak. And also showed that they would head east to the beach in search of salt to help her. It took several hours to finish, but when she stepped back to admire her work, she was proud of what she'd done.

In preparation for the new biome they were soon to be in, Stacy used her pocketknife to convert her jeans into cutoff shorts. As for her signature long-sleeved, blue-and-white-striped T-shirt, the elbows of which were patched and still threadbare . . . Stacy cut the bottom and the sleeves off to turn it into a cropped tank top. Springtime was pretty warm in the mesa, and Stacy suspected the beach would be even warmer. *I hope the beach is not full of people. I have a hard time making sure my six wolves stay undetected . . . now I'm supposed to hide eight?* Stacy pushed the thoughts out of her head. They didn't matter anyway, because Pearl was dying. Stacy was sure of it. But she was also sure that she would do whatever she had to do to keep Pearl alive. *I must think of some way to keep the wolves hidden. We can travel by night . . . and stay away from any villages . . . or . . . hmm, Everest was able to camouflage the other members of our pack when we were in the tundra. I wonder if he could do that to the members of the mesa pack too?* Everest barked and Stacy looked up to see him nodding at her. He walked over to Paisley, whose full body immediately turned the same clay color that stained her paws. She blended into the mesa perfectly. Paisley looked down at herself and got spooked. She ran from the red sand onto the stone floor of the mineshaft, her coat turning light gray to match the color of the andesite walls behind her. Paisley looked down at herself in wonder. Everest beamed with pride— his camouflage worked.

Perfect, Stacy thought. *This is how we'll get to the ocean.*

TEN

STACY GAZED OUT over the endless blue-gray ocean, her hair rippling in front of her eyes as the salty sea air swirled all around her. She was standing at the edge of a rocky cliff, with Page and Molly on either side of her. They'd arrived at the ocean biome only moments ago. It had taken the group three and a half days to make the southeasterly trek through the mesa, wetlands, and fen biomes to the rocky beach they were in now. They had been slowed down considerably by Pearl, who was now weaker than ever—and Page and Molly, who obviously could not run as fast as Stacy's wolves.

Stacy surveyed the coastline. To her left (north) there

was a small beach campground with several tents and firepits. There were people swimming in the surf near the campground. *We don't want to go up there, that's for sure.* Directly below Stacy was a jagged stretch of coast. Swells from the ocean crashed violently against the craggy cliffside. Stacy turned to the right (south) and spotted a small cove surrounded by thick brush and tall grass. *If we make our way down to that cove, I bet we'll get there as the tide goes out. That should be a secluded spot for us to spend the night and, most importantly, get Pearl into the salt water to soak.*

Suddenly, a strong gust of wind hit Stacy's back, toppling her forward. She stumbled toward the edge of the cliff and lost her footing, teetering back and forth just inches from falling. She waved her arms in frantic circles, trying to regain her balance, as Page and Molly looked up at her in helpless horror. Stacy was pitched forward so she could see the sharp rocky death that awaited her a hundred feet below. *At least it will be instant,* Stacy thought. But no sooner had the thought entered her mind, a second gust of wind—this one at least ten times stronger than the first—came from the opposite direction, hitting her directly in the stomach and knocking her backward. Stacy flew back six or seven feet away from the edge, coming down on her back. Her head jerked backward but was spared from hitting the rocks on the ground by another gust of wind that created an airy cushion between her body and the ground. She was fully suspended in the air for a split second before gently dropping a few inches down on the gravel.

Stacy sprang to her feet. *What just happened?* Then she turned around and saw him. *Atlas!* The massive wolf was standing right behind her, his soft fur billowing in the breeze. *Your power . . . it's the wind!*

Stacy was so relieved to be away from the edge of the cliff—and to finally know what Atlas's power was. She stepped up to him and extended her hand, which the large wolf met with his head. Stacy gave him a pat of deep gratitude and then ran back to where the others were standing.

"I'm okay, I'm okay," she said as she received wolf hugs from Everest, Wink, Basil, and Noah. "Thanks to Atlas—he saved me." Everest and the others nodded in appreciation to Atlas, who had returned to Pearl's side. Pearl was propped up between Paisley and Ribsy. Stacy walked over to her.

"Hang on just a little longer, girl," Stacy whispered in her ear. "We're here."

Stacy led everyone down a series of steep switchbacks toward the cove she'd seen from the top of the cliff. Just as she suspected, the tide was retreating as they made their way onto the secluded beach.

"Quick!" Stacy called to her pack. "Get Pearl into the ocean."

Everest, Atlas, Noah, and Wink carried Pearl down the beach and laid her in the surf. Stacy ran to catch up with them and bent down over Pearl's stiff body. It was lifeless.

"NO!!" Stacy sobbed. "Pearl, you can't die! Ribsy, quick, heal her!"

Ribsy lay down next to Pearl, and a small wave washed over them both. Seconds later, when the wave receded, Ribsy was gaunt—reduced to skin and bones again. Pearl was still motionless. Another second passed and suddenly she took a deep breath and snapped open her aquamarine eyes, a glimmer of hope shining brightly in them now.

"Pearl!" Stacy exclaimed. "Thank goodness!"

The sun began to set, and the quiet evening came to the little cove where Stacy, Page, Molly, and the wolves were huddled. Basil lit a bonfire on the beach, and Noah and Ribsy caught fish for the pack to eat for dinner. As they fished, Pearl swam tentatively around the cove, slowly regaining her strength. Ribsy had a unique way of killing fish—he caught them gently in his mouth and brought them to shore. Instead of flapping around wildly like the ones Noah caught, they seemed calm and still, as if in a trance. Ribsy bent down over each fish and seemed to almost suck the life right out of them. The fish died quickly and peacefully. *Incredible,* Stacy thought, as she and the others lounged on the beach. There was no need to build a shelter for the night to protect against the wind because it hadn't been blowing since they'd arrived in the cove—*That must be Atlas's work.*

Stacy sat in front of the bonfire, eating fresh-caught cod cooked and seasoned with wild fennel Paisley had foraged from the bluffs that surrounded the cove. Stacy looked around the circle of animals she was with, staring for a long time at Atlas, Paisley, and Ribsy—her new pack members. Stacy didn't know what the future held. *What happened to these wolves' parents? Would the mesa pack want to come home to the taiga with us? If Pearl heals, will she need to stay close to the ocean?* Stacy didn't know the answers to these questions, but she was so grateful to have found the wolves. Stacy stood and walked down the beach to where Pearl was swimming and threw her a piece of fish. Pearl caught it in her mouth and swallowed it.

"Get some good rest tonight, will you?" Stacy said to her before heading back up the beach to where the others were bedding down for the night. She fell asleep against Wink and Paisley, looking up at the stars until she could no longer keep her eyes open.

Stacy woke up rather abruptly the next morning when a big clump of sand hit her in the face.

"Plthhhh . . . ppppthhhhh," Stacy sputtered as she sat up and spat the sand out of her mouth. She looked over to see Molly happily digging on the beach, unaware that she was kicking sand up onto Stacy.

"Molly!" Stacy shouted. "Stop!" The little dog whipped around and cocked her head, looking at her owner for a second before happily running over to greet Stacy. Molly's nose was covered in sand, and she was panting heavily. Stacy couldn't possibly be mad at her.

"Are you enjoying the beach, girl?" Stacy cooed at Molly. "Or, at least, the sand part of the beach. I know you're still a bit leery of the water."

Stacy got up and stretched. She looked at all her wolves who were sleeping around her—still tired from the journey to the ocean. Page was running along the shore chasing seagulls. She looked as if she was having the time of her life. Stacy walked over to the only two wolves who weren't dozing: Atlas and Pearl. Atlas was watching Pearl from the beach. Stacy waded into the water up to her knees to get closer to Pearl, who was swimming in large circles around the cove. Stacy noticed that Pearl was swimming slightly faster than she had been able to the previous evening. And her fur was looking shiny and smooth. *Maybe I was right, after all. Maybe the ocean can heal her.*

Stacy left Atlas and Pearl and walked with Molly over toward where Page was playing on the beach, where the cove gave way to a jumble of rocks and small tide pools. Stacy climbed over the rocks with Page and Molly and set off on a walk on the other side of the cove—she figured she could explore a little, while all the wolves rested. The sun was just beginning to poke out over the horizon of the ocean. Now that Stacy was here, she was quite certain that the beach she had visited before had been a great big lake and not an ocean. For starters, the beach she had been to before was filled only with smooth rocks and driftwood. She had never experienced sand like this before. She loved the way it felt as she squished her toes down into it. And there were lots of other things here that she didn't remember seeing on that trip. *Seashells! Sand dollars! And starfish! And all the—yeeeeeooooowwwww!* Stacy looked down at the small red crab who had locked onto her toe with its right claw.

"Get off of me, you crusty crab!" Stacy yelled in pain.

She didn't want to hurt the crab, but she now wished she hadn't left her boots back at the cove where her wolves were sleeping. Fortunately, the crab released its grip, and Stacy hopped away. Page growled at the crab ferociously.

"It's fine, Page," Stacy said. "Just leave him."

Stacy, Page, and Molly continued walking across the rocky beach at the edge of the cove and eventually came to a point where the beach widened again. Stacy looked back toward the cove, which was now completely hidden from view. *We can go a little bit farther. We're not that far away really.*

Stacy picked up a piece of driftwood and threw the stick as far as she could down the beach. Page and Molly took off running after it, with Page easily winning the race and bringing the stick back to Stacy. Meanwhile, Molly seemed to forget what she was doing midway down the beach and began barking at a pile of seaweed that had washed up on the shore. Stacy played fetch with Page for a long time while Molly gnawed on seaweed pods. And when Page got tired, all of them sat down in the sand and watched the waves roll in. Stacy studied the birds of the beach biome intently. There were the seagulls who glided slowly around above her head, catching rides on waves of wind. There were pelicans who periodically dove into the water for fish. And dozens of little sandpipers ran down the beach as the waves receded, looking for tiny insects to eat—only to race back up the sand as the next wave arrived. Stacy's mind wandered as she watched the birds.

If the ocean heals Pearl . . . she'll have to stay here. And her pack members will want to stay with her. Could we move here? Leave the taiga? It's always been my home, but for as long as I can remember, the villagers have been trying to force me out of it. First, they came and hunted the wolves, then there was the construction company that attempted to demolish it. Now the wolf researchers are constantly poking around for new subjects to study . . . not to mention the steady flow of hikers and campers . . . and the forest fire that almost destroyed everything. What if we moved here? Page and Molly seem to love it. But what about Milquetoast and Pipsqueak? I can't imagine a cat living on a beach. And what if Addison and Tucker don't like it here? And what about Miriam and her offer to send me to school . . . and Dr. Kay and the hospital bill I need to work off . . . and Ezra and the animal shelter I can volunteer at?

Stacy realized she was staring at something in the distance, bobbing on the ocean's surface. *What is that?* Whatever it was, it sank under the water briefly and then, a moment later, resurfaced. Stacy jumped up. *Is it an animal?* She squinted—the morning sun was reflecting off the water, making it impossible for Stacy to know for sure. Something didn't feel right to Stacy about the way it jerked around helplessly in the water.

"I'm pretty sure it's an animal," Stacy said to Page and Molly as she lifted her satchel's strap above her head, flung it to the ground, and started running into the surf. "And I think it's in trouble!"

ELEVEN

STACY GASPED WHEN the cold water slapped up against her legs as she ran into the waves. A shiver started up her body, but before it could reach her waist, Stacy dove into a coming wave, soaking her entire body. She came up for a gulp of air and then began swimming as quickly as she could toward the animal.

I should have known I'd find an animal to rescue here at the beach. . . . I seem to find one no matter where I go.

She swam for a minute or two and then glanced behind her as she continued to paddle. She could see Page and Molly far in the distance, looking nervously at her from the beach. Stacy hadn't meant to go out this far into the ocean, but the animal kept swimming farther away—it was obviously weak and being pushed out with the current. Stacy stuck her head down in the water and swam as fast as she could for the length of another breath. She blew bubbles out through her nose and paddled vigorously until she needed to come up for more air. When she broke through the water, she saw that she was an arm's length away from her rescue target, but that the animal she'd seen from the beach wasn't an animal at all. It was a tangle of trash. Just some aluminum cans, plastic bags, and candy wrappers—all held together by a twisted knot of twine and seaweed.

Trash? Why would there be a bunch of trash floating in the ocean? Stacy reached her arms out and turned the garbage over in the water, examining it. *The campers up the shore!* Stacy was so angry. *I swam all the way out here for nothing? Just to . . . to rescue a pile of litter!* She calmed herself by thinking about how it was actually a very good thing that there wasn't an animal who needed rescuing, but she was still upset about it. And exhausted too. In fact, Stacy was so tired from the swim out that even treading water was proving difficult for her. Stacy looked back at the beach where Page and Molly were. They were just tiny specks on the sand now. She was so far out in the ocean! Stacy swallowed the little lump of panic that bubbled up inside of her. *It's fine. I'll just swim back to shore now.* Stacy began paddling back toward the coast, but no matter how hard she swam, she kept getting pushed farther and farther out to sea. *What's happening? Am I just too tired?* Stacy's legs and arms ached, but she kept swimming, determined to get back to Page and Molly. Another minute passed and Stacy looked up to see she wasn't any closer. She stopped swimming and decided to tread water for a bit to regain some energy before swimming again. But even dog-paddling was too hard for her now. The water was pushing her backward. *I think I'm in a rip current!* Suddenly, Stacy's arms gave out from exertion, and she dipped below the surface, completely submerged for a moment before bobbing up again and gasping for air. Both her throat and nose burned from swallowing salt water.

"Help!" Stacy managed to shout, but she realized there was no one around to hear her. She slipped under the water again, this time for several seconds more than the first. *I . . . I think I'm drowning. Everest! Everest, can you hear me?* Stacy managed to come up for air again, splashing wildly—unable to see which direction the beach was anymore. Everything around her was blue.

"Page!" Stacy managed to sputter. "Page, get Noa-bluhhbluhh!"

Stacy sank under the water once more. She wasn't sure if she would be able to swim back up to the surface for air this time. *Everest might still be asleep and unable to hear my thoughts. I should never have come out here without my wolves. I didn't know the ocean was so strong.*

Stacy forced her eyes open under the water. It stung briefly, but then she could see around her. She could see the ripples of the rip current she was fighting, and how it was pushing her away from the land. Out of the corner of her eye, she also saw a familiar white shape speeding toward her under the waves. *Noah!*

Stacy reached out and grabbed onto Noah's back, and he pulled her up to the surface. She took a huge breath of air and tightened her grip around the wolf's neck.

"Noah!" Stacy gasped. She was so relieved Page had been able to get Noah to save her. But no sooner had Stacy taken another deep breath in than a large wave came and crashed over them both, sending them tumbling underwater. Stacy was pushed and pulled by the water just like the pile of trash had been, completely powerless to the churning of the ocean. She looked over to Noah, whose face had an unfamiliar expression of panic on it. Noah swam toward Stacy, and she grabbed hold of his fur once again as he fought in vain against the current before relenting and allowing it to push them back again.

Stacy had never seen Noah like this in the water. It appeared—even though he was the best swimmer of the pack and could hold his breath for as long as he wanted— he was no match for the sheer power of the ocean. Still, Noah continued to paddle as hard as he could, desperate to save Stacy.

Stacy couldn't believe how foolish she had been. She did not have a backup plan. Noah had been her only hope. And if he couldn't save her in these waters, Stacy was sure that Everest, Basil, or Wink wouldn't be able to either. Their best chance of survival would be letting the current take them wherever it wanted to—and hoping they were lucky enough to wash up on the beach some-where, instead of being carried farther out to sea . . . or down to the bottom of the ocean.

Suddenly, Stacy looked up and saw a graceful white figure jumping effortlessly over the rip current and diving below them. *Was that? It couldn't be . . . Pearl?!* Stacy looked down in the water as Pearl zoomed around underneath them until she popped up directly between Stacy and Noah. Stacy blinked several times to make sure she hadn't just swallowed too much salt water and her eyes were playing tricks on her.

Pearl looked like a completely different wolf. Her fur was longer and wavy and flowed around her beautifully in the water. And the way she glided through the ocean was so different from how Noah swam. She used her hind legs and tail together as one powerful muscle to propel her through the water like a fish, or a dolphin, or . . . a mermaid! Pearl gave Stacy and Noah a salty lick on the face and then shook the excess water from her head. Stacy and Noah exchanged puzzled looks with each other but shrugged and held on to either side of Pearl as the graceful wolf swam them down-current through the riptide and over to the beach where all the other wolves and Page and Molly were anxiously waiting. As they approached the shore, Pearl caught a wave and rode it onto the beach, with Stacy and Noah clinging to either side of her. Pearl made the transition from swimming in the water to running on the sand with delicate ease, leaving Stacy and Noah sprawled out on the beach on their bellies, panting heavily.

"Pearl is . . . amazing," Stacy managed between breaths. "Did you all see her? She saved us." Stacy looked around at the others—Everest, Basil, Wink, Ribsy, Paisley, and Atlas—and saw that they all had different reactions to Pearl's transformation, ranging from astonished to impressed to downright disbelieving. Page and Molly ran over to Stacy and Noah to make sure they were all right. Stacy comforted them.

"I'm okay, I'm okay," Stacy said, gently stroking Page and Molly on the head and taking back her satchel from where it was hanging around Page's neck. "Page, you saved the day in alerting Noah. And then Pearl saved both of us—well, me at least—from drowning."

Stacy took a minute before she could get up, but eventually she stood and wrung out her wet hair. Everest walked over, carrying Stacy's pair of boots and her flannel shirt in his mouth.

"Thanks, boy," Stacy said, taking the boots and the shirt from Everest's jaw and putting them on. Her cutoff shorts and tank top were still soaked, but the flannel provided some warmth against her freezing skin.

Stacy walked over to where Pearl was standing. Stacy couldn't believe what she was seeing. Pearl looked one hundred percent better. Stacy surveyed their surroundings. The rip current had pushed them much farther south than where she'd started from, and they were on a completely different part of the beach now, probably almost a mile from the cove where they'd spent the previous night. This part of the beach was rockier and looked like it would be completely underwater when the tide came in. Stacy wasn't sure what their plans were for the rest of the day now that Pearl was feeling better, but she knew that she and Noah needed to rest and that this probably wasn't a safe spot to do so. She was just about to suggest they all head back to the cove when something on the beach caught her eye.

"Oh wow," she gasped. "I . . . I don't believe it!"

Stacy was looking at something up the beach when, suddenly, a loud male voice boomed behind them in the ocean.

"Over there! On the beach! What are those?"

TWELVE

STACY, PAGE, AND Molly dove behind a large boulder to hide while Everest camouflaged himself and the other wolves—taking on the various shades of grays and blues of the rocks on the ground. Stacy peeked around the boulder to see two kayakers paddling in the ocean exactly where she herself had been just minutes before.

"I saw something right here," said the villager in a red kayak. "A big group of wolves or something."

"Wolves?" asked the villager in the green kayak skeptically. "I don't see any wolves."

"Okay then, dogs maybe," the red kayaker replied.

"Don't see any dogs either."

Stacy ducked back down behind the boulder as the villagers paddled toward the rocks for a closer look. Her heart was beating so loud she worried the kayakers would hear it and get out of their boats to investigate. She had made the mistake of thinking her pack would be safe this far south of the beach campground. She had forgotten all the different ways people could still get close to them in the water, like catamarans, canoes, and kayaks.

"They were here just a second ago," the red kayaker said. Stacy could hear their voices much clearer now, which meant they were extremely close.

"How would a group of dogs even get here?" the green kayaker countered. "They must have been birds; what did they look like?"

The villagers continued their back-and-forth about what birds Stacy's wolves might have been, with the villager in the green kayak naming large white species like pelicans, herons, and cranes while the villager in the red kayak continued to insist he had seen dogs, not birds.

Stacy was relieved when their voices began to trail off as they paddled away, and Everest and the other wolves reappeared in front of her. She let out a big sigh of relief and instantly remembered what she had been so excited about just moments ago. She scrambled across the rocky beach to the opening of a small sea cave.

"Look!" she shouted to her wolves.

Poking out of the sea cave, just far enough for Stacy to spot it, was a dilapidated sailboat—broken, rusty, and complete with a tattered sail. *Is this boat irreparably broken, or could it still sail?*

Stacy and her pack clambered over the rocky shore to get closer to the cave. Three other thoughts ran through Stacy's mind. The first and most practical thought was that Stacy had just found her pack shelter for the night. They could sleep in the boat, and then they'd be safe even when the tide came in. This would probably be a safer place to spend the night than in the cove. Stacy hadn't realized how exposed they had been to villagers like the kayakers.

Stacy's second thought was a bit more complicated. *If Pearl needs to live near the ocean, I might have just found Atlas, Ribsy, and Paisley their new home. We could fix it up for them just like we fixed up our cave back in the taiga, and they could all live here with her.* Stacy imagined using her pickaxe to mine a ledge in the back of the cave where Ribsy, Atlas, and Paisley could sleep when the tide came in. She could use the wolf saddlebag to have Wink carry in bags of the cove's soft sand that she could pour down for the wolves to sleep on. And she envisioned making a curtain out of seaweed and kelp that they could hide behind if anyone tried to explore the cave. *What a fun project!*

Stacy's third (and a bit crazy if she was being honest with herself) thought lingered in the back of her mind and was more complicated still. *If I could repair the boat, then maybe we would be able to learn how to sail it. And if that happened . . . then we could go anywhere! We could sail north toward the taiga and the tundra. Maybe we could even find the Arctic explorer!*

Everest barked, which Stacy took as a gentle warning to not get too ahead of herself. The group waded into the sea cave to where the boat was swaying back and forth in about a foot of water. There was a large crack in its hull from jostling on the rocks in the cave—*that would need to be repaired.* Stacy ran her fingers along the crack. *I bet we could find some natural materials here on the beach to fix this.* Next, Stacy climbed onto Basil's back and then grabbed on to the boat and pulled herself up onto its small deck. Stacy turned to see Atlas jump aboard the boat in a single, swift leap. Stacy was pretty sure none of her wolves could jump that high. While the others waited down in the water, exploring the sea cave, Stacy and Atlas took stock of the wooden sailboat. The deck was weathered and worn, but it was otherwise in working condition. The sail was mildewy and ripped. Stacy walked toward the boat's helm and put her hand on the wooden steering wheel. *The boat isn't in bad shape! We probably could fix it up and use it! I don't know anything about sailing, but how hard could it be?* Stacy opened the door to a stairway that descended into a tiny cabin. There was a wooden table and bench built into the boat's wall, a small kitchen area with a few cupboards and drawers, as well as a low platform with a few cushions on it—also mildewy. Above the platform was a round porthole, big enough for Stacy to climb and sit in. *How cool would it be to have a boat! I wonder if we could sail all the way up to the Arctic?* Stacy collected what she could find from the cupboards and drawers and laid it on the big wooden table for herself and Atlas to examine: a soggy map, an emergency flare, a cooking pot, a yellow rain jacket, a red-and-white-striped life preserver, two orange life jackets, a box of nails, and a pair of swimming goggles.

Stacy brought the soggy map upstairs with her to the deck and found that a few of her wolves had made their way onto the boat as well. Everest was sniffing around while Wink was tangled up in the sail. Stacy laid the wet map out on the wooden planks of the deck's floor and inspected it. She instantly recognized that the map's topography was of this region. She saw the beach campground, the rocky point, the small inlet where the cove was, the stone beach she was on now, and then she could also see farther out into the ocean to the east. There looked to be a cluster of tiny islands a few miles out to sea.

"There," Stacy said, pointing to the islands. "We could sail to there."

Atlas nodded and studied the map as if he were committing it to memory. Meanwhile, Everest bristled at Stacy's suggestion. He shot Stacy a concerned look.

Everest. You saw how close those kayakers came to spotting us just then. In fact, they did *spot us. What if you hadn't been here to camouflage Pearl and the others? She needs to stay near the ocean, but it's too risky for her and the rest of the mesa pack to live at the beach. Even if they lived in this cave, there's no guarantee that people won't find them eventually. An island, though? That would be perfect. They'll have everything they need to live on an island. Paisley can grow food and Ribsy knows how to fish. We can come back and visit them whenever we want! We just need to get this boat fixed up so we can sail there and back.*

Stacy hopped down off the boat and walked over to where everyone else was hanging out in the back of the sea cave. Atlas, Everest, and Wink followed her. She explained to Noah and Basil what she had been discussing with Everest. And then Everest came over and translated what she had said to the other members of the mesa pack. Stacy looked around the group—one by one, their tails began to wag until everyone was wagging their tails and pawing at the ground in eager excitement.

"Okay, so we're all in agreement then," Stacy said, turning back to face the rickety vessel. "We've got a boat to fix!"

THIRTEEN

STACY AND HER wolves wasted no time in beginning to repair the abandoned sailboat. The first thing they needed to do was to prop the boat up to keep it from rocking as ocean water sloshed around the rocks of the cave. Everest and Atlas dragged huge driftwood logs over as Wink positioned himself under the boat to lift it with his back. Wink lifted each side of the boat just long enough for Everest and Atlas to push the driftwood under the boat. They worked quickly, and the boat was soon stabilized. Stacy had them bring another driftwood log over to lean up against the boat. Using her knife, she carved horizontal notches into the wood about a foot apart from each other so that she (and Page and Molly) would be able to quickly climb up onto the deck of the boat and back down to the cave floor.

While Paisley went off to find some materials to patch the crack in the side of the boat, Stacy took down the sail and removed the mildewy cushions from the pillows in the cabin and carried them down the beach to rinse them off. Page and Molly accompanied her, chasing gulls along the rocky shoreline. Pearl was already there, swimming happily in the ocean. Page dove into the water to swim with her. Stacy set about washing the sail and the cushions while keeping a watchful eye on Page as she tried her best to keep up with Pearl, who was swimming circles around her. Molly stayed on the shore, running away from the waves as they rolled in. *Wait a minute, what am I thinking? I can't put Molly on a boat and sail into the middle of the ocean if she refuses to swim. I don't know if she even knows how!* Stacy looked at the little dog.

"Okay, Molly," she said in a calm voice. "You're going to have your first swimming lesson today."

Stacy set her washing aside on some rocks to dry and ran back to the boat. She scurried up the driftwood log with the notches and climbed down into the boat's cabin and retrieved the swimming goggles she'd found. *These are obviously meant for a human, but who says I can't use them on a dog?* Stacy walked back down to the beach where Molly was sitting. She bent down and delicately strapped the goggles around the dog's head, tucking the strap under her floppy ears. Page and Pearl swam over to see what Stacy was doing.

"Pearl!" Stacy said with a sudden dawn of realization. "You can help me, actually!"

Stacy stood and picked Molly up, placing her on top of Pearl's back.

"There you go, Molly," Stacy cooed. "Pearl is going to take you for a little ride, nothing to be afraid of."

Molly glared up at Stacy as Pearl set off on a slow swim in the calm ocean. Pearl made a couple of gentle turns, keeping Molly above the water.

"It's okay, Molly!" Stacy called to the little dog, who was clinging to Pearl like her life depended on it. "You're doing great!"

Suddenly, a mischievous grin appeared on Pearl's face. She dove down under the water. Molly hit the water with all four of her paws and began to swim wildly. Stacy and Page cheered from the shore until they realized the little dog was sinking. Luckily, Pearl acted fast and swam under Molly as she sank, and pushed her up to the surface. Molly lay splayed out on Pearl's back as the mermaid-like wolf swam back to the shore.

Molly stumbled off Pearl's back and collapsed dramatically onto the beach. When she noticed that Stacy and Page were unfazed by her performance, she stood up and shook off for what seemed to Stacy to be an entire minute. Water droplets flew from Molly's gigantic ears as she turned her head in circles, flapping them. The goggles flew off and landed several feet away from Molly. Then she walked forward, shaking her entire body and wiggling her butt rapidly.

"Are you okay, Molly?" Stacy asked earnestly.

The little dog offered a snort and then smugly walked up the beach and onto the sailboat.

Stacy sighed and bent down to pick up the goggles. "I guess we won't be trying that again anytime soon."

Stacy and Page walked back up into the sea cave to find Paisley and Basil huddled around a fire. On top of it was the cooking pot from the boat.

"Ooh, whatcha making?" Stacy asked. "Is this lunch?"

Stacy bent over the pot and took a deep breath in and recoiled in disgust. Inside the pot was a disgusting stew of mussels and slimy kelp. Paisley stirred the sticky concoction with a branch. *There is no way I'm eating that.* Just then, Stacy looked over at Noah, who had brought a bunch of clay he'd found around the beach over to the side of the boat with the large crack in it. A wave of realization washed over Stacy. *Oh! Oh! Paisley is making a glue for the crack. Genius! We can fill the crack with the clay—it will harden and expand as it dries, and then we can seal it with Paisley's glue!*

Stacy and the wolves repaired the crack until the sun began to set. They sat back and admired their work while Page and Molly napped and Ribsy brought fresh-caught fish for supper into the cave.

A couple days passed. The days were short and consisted mainly of working on the boat, late-night bonfires on the beach, and early-morning dips in the ocean when it was more likely there wouldn't be villagers nearby. Stacy slept in the tiny cabin on the boat along with Page, Molly, Wink, Paisley, and Ribsy. The other wolves— Everest, Atlas, Basil, and Noah—preferred to sleep on the deck of the boat. And Pearl, of course, liked sleeping on a flat rock at the base of the boat, where she could dip into a pool of water whenever she felt like it.

Stacy finished repairing all the tears in the sail, and Noah and Atlas helped her fasten it back on the boat. She'd spent a few hours carving a rune into the wall of the sea cave explaining where they intended to sail.

She also made several attempts to get Molly back in the water for swimming practice, but each attempt was met with an increasing level of resistance. Stacy wasn't sure if she should force Molly into the water or give up altogether and just adapt one of the boat's life jackets to fit the small dog. But then, one morning, Stacy awoke with a thought in her head that she absolutely hated at first. But as the sun rose and the idea sank in, Stacy realized it was the only way. *Basil should take Page and Molly back to the taiga, Everest. I've been thinking about it, and it's not safe for them to come with us. Basil is so fast! If we secure both dogs on either side of her in the saddlebag, they could all be back in the taiga in time for whatever Addison is making for dinner tonight. It will be safer for them than coming with us. You know I'm right.*

Everest came and sat down beside Stacy. She could tell he was mulling over everything Stacy had been thinking. *We could even send Wink with them for added protection,* Stacy added in case Everest wasn't convinced.

Basil would have to run a bit slower, but they'd be safe together. Think about it . . . your camouflage power and Noah's underwater breathing will both come in handy on our trip. But speed and invincibility . . . those aren't really things we need on an island surrounded by the ocean.

Everest nodded glumly. Stacy knew he wasn't too keen on the idea. After all, Stacy couldn't think of a time when she had been separated from her wolves like this. For as long as she could remember, it had been just her and her pack of six wolves in the taiga. But now they'd been away from Addison and Tucker for a considerable amount of time—and were going to separate from Wink and Basil. Stacy was comforted by the knowledge that the separation wouldn't be for long. She would go and get the mesa pack settled on an island in the ocean and then return to the taiga as soon as possible. It would be summer soon, and Stacy had decided she would love nothing more than to work at the animal hospital and volunteer at the animal shelter in the village. She couldn't wait to learn from Dr. Kay and Ezra. As for school in the fall, she still wasn't sure how she felt about it. But having a nice summer in the taiga—with Page, Molly, Milquetoast, Pipsqueak, and all six wolves—sounded like the best thing in the world to her right now.

Stacy spent the rest of the morning reinforcing the

pack that Basil would wear to carry Page and Molly. Stacy knew that Page was a few pounds heavier than Molly, so she sewed a small pocket in Molly's side of the pack where she could store a few items to distribute the weight evenly on Basil's back. This would help Basil run faster. Inside of it, Stacy placed a few pebbles and shells from the beach—the pebbles were just to add some extra weight to Molly's side, but the shells she wanted back at the cave, so she could display them on her bookshelf and remember her time living at the ocean. She also added a few fish-skin treats for them to eat on the way. *I'm not sure packing these in Molly's side is a smart idea. I hope Page gets at least a couple of them and Molly doesn't just help herself.*

And then—whether Stacy liked it or not—it was time for Page, Molly, Basil, and Wink to head home to the taiga. Stacy walked with them to the little cove where they had spent their first night at the beach. Everest and Noah came along to say their good-byes as well. Even though it had been her idea, Stacy hated saying good-bye to these members of her pack, and she started to cry. She bent down to hug them each.

"Page, tell Milo to send word via the bats that you all made it home safe," Stacy said, scratching behind the dog's ears. "And give Addison, Tucker, and the cats lots of kisses from me."

Stacy, Everest, and Noah watched for as long as they could as Basil and Wink climbed out of the cove, up the switchbacks, and out of their sight. Stacy, Everest, and Noah returned to the sea cave where the mesa pack was hanging out—all the work on the boat was complete. They had a quiet supper and an even quieter evening. Stacy didn't realize how much she would miss Page and Molly—and also how noticeable it was that Wink and Basil (the two goofballs of her pack) were absent. She decided to go to bed in the ship's cabin early and decode more of the tundra explorer's journal.

We arrived in the tundra late last night to what can only be described as a bittersweet discovery. Diamond is pregnant again. This is, of course, thrilling news as it means we will soon have even more wolves with, we can only presume, more unique abilities. It presents a rather dire logistical problem, however, as the tundra is severely lacking in resources these days. The current litter is not even a year old and growing fast. Without any other adult pack members to lighten the load, it's far too much work for Ames to

*provide for five young pups and another litter
on the way. My first inclination is to relocate
the pups. Yes, they are young. But they are
gifted, after all, and they have each other.
If we move them while they are young, they
will adapt. We are taking a very hands-off
approach to interacting with the pups now,
as we want them to be self-sufficient and
slightly apprehensive of humans. The nearby
taiga would be an excellent home biome for
the pack: plenty of food and shelter. It should
be easy for them to survive, and thrive, there.
And we will be able to check in on them,
from a distance, and intervene if necessary.*

Stacy read the journal entry a second time. And then she read it a third. *This is it. Finally. This is the answer to how my pack of Arctic wolves came to the taiga.* It was a piece of the story Stacy had been missing for so long, but now that she had it—she wanted more. She was desperate to keep reading, but her eyes—tired from swimming and crying that day—could not stay open another minute. Stacy blew out her candle and tried to quiet her mind. But she knew that sleep would not come easily.

FOURTEEN

STACY WOKE UP. It was still dark out, but she was surprised to see that Atlas, Ribsy, Everest, and Paisley had managed to lift the boat off the driftwood logs as the morning tide came in. *They want to leave? Now?* Stacy hesitated . . . she knew today was the day they should try to sail toward the little islands on the map. The weather had been calm last night, and with Page and Molly gone and Pearl completely healed, there was nothing standing in their way. Stacy hadn't planned on setting sail for the islands until the sun had come up and they could see where they were going, but now that she thought about it, it was smarter to do it in the cover of darkness, to be sure they didn't run into any other ships. *Besides, who knows if I'll even be able to get the boat to work. This may end up being just a practice run.*

Stacy donned the yellow rain jacket, as the sun was still not up and Tucker was not around to make the boat's cabin warm. Stacy wished Tucker was there just as much as she wished Addison was with her. *Addison would know how to sail this boat better than me. She would have read something in a book sometime or at least have better instincts about it. I don't know what I'm doing.*

Stacy climbed the couple stairs from the boat's tiny cabin and looked around the sea cave. The tide was high, causing the boat to rise in the water to the point where its mast was almost poking the top of the cave. Everest and Noah were pulling up the boat's anchor that had been keeping it in the cave. The boat began to glide out of the cave with the current, and with one last powerful tug, the two wolves heaved the heavy metal anchor on deck.

Stacy's legs wobbled as the boat rocked up and down with the ocean's powerful early morning waves. She grabbed onto the closest wolf to her—Ribsy's bony frame—and steadied herself. *What am I doing? I don't have the foggiest clue how to captain a sailboat. I'm going to get us all killed.* Just as Stacy was about to tell her wolves that she wanted to literally jump ship, Atlas sprang into action. He unfurled the boat's sail and instructed Noah to tie a knot at the base of the mast.

"Atlas!" Stacy exclaimed. "Of course!" Atlas took his position at the front of the boat and filled the sail with a powerful gust of wind. The boat surged forward, cutting forcefully through the water. Stacy was amazed and let out a huge sigh of relief. *Atlas can do this. He can control the wind! He can do things like use the wind to jump really, really high or send a gust of wind to push me backward to save me from falling off a cliff. Of course he can fill a sail with it too!*

Stacy looked behind her as they sailed away from the coast. She could still see the small sea cave, the cove, the rocky point, and the villagers' beach, but all those landmarks appeared smaller and smaller by the minute. She looked above the cove to the series of switchbacks that Basil and Wink had run up on their way home to the taiga. Stacy felt a little nervous about traveling even farther away from her home—and from Page and Molly, who were probably already back in the cave with Milquetoast and Pipsqueak—but Stacy knew she would be safe with her wolves. And by that, Stacy wasn't just thinking about Everest and Noah. Sure, she felt completely safe in their company. She always had. But she also felt safe with Atlas, Ribsy, Paisley, and Pearl. They were part of her crazy wolf family now—a fact that Stacy couldn't be happier about.

Stacy looked one more time at the fading coastline in the distance and then reached over and hugged Paisley as she turned to face the rising sun. Stacy squinted to look around the boat at her new pack. Paisley was standing next to Stacy, her bandanna rippling in the wind. Atlas worked the sail while Everest stood near the ship's wheel, guiding it every so often to keep the boat on course. Noah was at the very front of the boat, basking in all the water droplets that were spraying up in his face. Ribsy was lounging in the ship's cabin. Stacy turned around in a full circle. *Someone is missing. Wait . . . where's Pearl?*

Stacy ran into the cabin to see if Pearl was hiding on the bench or somewhere Stacy couldn't see from the deck. But only Ribsy was down there, sprawled out on the cushions Stacy had cleaned. Stacy was about to rush back out onto the deck to tell Atlas that Pearl was missing when something caught her eye. She climbed up into the large porthole above the platform that Ribsy was sleeping on and pressed her nose to the glass. There was Pearl, swimming alongside the boat, weaving gracefully through schools of fish and stingrays. *Wow. She really is like a mermaid.* Stacy happily sat curled up in the porthole watching Pearl swim for what must have been close to an hour. The agile wolf never tired, and Stacy never tired of taking in all of the interesting marine life they were passing: jellyfish, cuttlefish, sand tiger sharks, and eels. Suddenly, several gray shapes appeared swimming next to her. Stacy focused her eyes and gasped. *Dolphins!* A pod of ten or fifteen dolphins caught up to the sailboat and began swimming around it. Stacy ran out of the cabin and onto the deck just in time to see one of the dolphins from the pod leap out of the water and jump completely over the bow of the boat. Mouth agape, Stacy watched the dolphin as it soared in the air. Pearl followed the dolphin's lead and also jumped out of the water and over the sailboat. Stacy almost couldn't believe it. But of course, she did believe it. These wolves were incredible and, as far as Stacy was concerned, there was nothing they couldn't do.

Atlas lowered the sail and slowed the boat down while Noah jumped into the ocean to join Pearl and the dolphins. The pod stayed with the boat for twenty minutes or so, and in that time, Stacy and the other wolves were so busy watching Pearl and Noah playing in the ocean with the dolphins that they didn't look up once. If they had, they surely would have seen the ominous black clouds roll in and the lightning striking the ocean in the distance. . . .

FIFTEEN

BEFORE STACY COULD retrieve the life jacket from the boat's cabin, the storm was upon them. The deck of the boat was slick with rainwater, and Stacy knew if she tried to maneuver toward the stairs, she'd slip and fall. She feared for her life like she never had before. She was more scared than when the taiga forest had been engulfed in flames. More panicked than when an avalanche swept her hundreds of feet off a cliff and buried her under snow. And more frightened than she'd been when she was staring down the barrel of a farmer's shotgun. Because right now, Stacy and her wolves were completely at the mercy of the sea. There was nothing they could do to escape the huge waves that were crashing down on top of the boat's deck. All they could do was ride out the storm and hope they survived.

The small sailboat rocked back and forth wildly as it was pummeled by one huge wave after another. Noah and Pearl watched in horror from the sea as they swam alongside the boat, waiting to see if Stacy or one of the wolves was going to fall overboard and need rescuing. Stacy was relieved that Ribsy and Paisley were safe at least—they were huddled together in the ship's small cabin. On the deck, Atlas was doing all he could to keep the sail from being torn to shreds in the storm's fierce winds. Stacy was at the wheel of the boat, trying in vain to keep it sailing in a straight line. Everest stood behind her, keeping Stacy secure between him and the wheel, but every couple minutes, a giant wave would come crashing down and send them sliding backward on the deck. They'd spend the next minute fighting their way back to the wheel only to repeat the process a minute later.

"Rocks ahead!" Stacy screamed at the top of her lungs to Everest and Atlas. *Those weren't on the map,* Stacy thought to herself as she caught glimpses of the formidable rocks in between the wave's sizable swells. *I'll have to try to steer the boat around them!* Stacy turned the boat's wheel just in time to narrowly avoid the first large rock.

Yes! Maybe I can do this! She wiped the rain and wet hair away from her eyes and looked ahead.

A bolt of lightning struck the water in the distance, illuminating a maze of rocks looming in front of them. *On second thought . . . maybe I can't.* C-C-C-R-A-C-K. The boat rammed into one of the rocks. Stacy, Everest, and Atlas all slid across the deck, nearly falling overboard altogether. They managed to get up and back to their positions, only to hit another rock head on. Ribsy and Paisley were barking down in the cabin. Stacy glanced over the side of the boat to see they had begun kicking water out of the boat's broken porthole. *We're taking on water. We're going to sink. What was I thinking trying to sail a boat in the first place? I'm not strong enough to help Atlas.*

Suddenly, lightning struck the boat's mast, splitting it in half. Atlas commanded a gust of wind to keep the mast from falling directly onto them while Everest grabbed Stacy by her raincoat and pulled her overboard. Stacy looked below her to see Paisley and Ribsy jumping out of the boat's porthole as she and Everest plunged into the cold water alongside them. The boat was heading directly toward more rocks; there was nothing they could do to save it.

Stacy held on as Everest pulled her deeper and deeper

underwater, away from the storm's turbulent waves on the surface. Stacy knew this was wise, to avoid the crashing waves and their out-of-control boat, but she also knew that she needed to come up for air soon. *I can't hold my breath as long as you, Everest. What are you doing?* Stacy looked to her right to see Atlas was swimming beside her and Everest. Together they were guiding Stacy over to where the water was much calmer. Stacy tried to kick away from them to paddle up for a breath, but she was sandwiched between the two wolves. *I'm going to drown!* Stacy held her breath for as long as she could, about a minute, and then started frantically puffing her cheeks out and in. Everything had happened so fast in the chaos of the storm; Stacy didn't know what was going on. She was losing consciousness. *Everest must have forgotten I can't hold my breath as long as him. . . .* Stacy couldn't last another second. She closed her eyes and opened her mouth to accept her watery fate. Stacy expected salt water to enter her mouth, filling her throat and burning its way into her lungs. But instead, her mouth was filled with a gulp of sweet ocean air. *What . . . is . . . happening?* Stacy looked over at Atlas. He was swimming incredibly close to her. *I can . . . I can breathe? Underwater? Atlas can keep air . . . around him?* Stacy couldn't fully appreciate this new development in Atlas's powers. In her mind, she was still back on the deck of the boat, trying desperately to steer around rocks. Her brain could not keep up with her body and the fact that she was now hurtling through the turbulent ocean waters. Stacy, Everest, and Atlas surfaced, and through the rain, Stacy could see land up ahead. A wave, at least twenty feet tall, crashed over them, knocking Stacy away from Everest and Atlas. Stacy was pushed under the water and felt a sharp pain in her leg and then a tug on the hood of her raincoat. She looked around to see Pearl, pulling her toward the shore.

Stacy stumbled onto the shore and collapsed on the soft sand. She turned onto her back, gasping for air, and saw that the dark rain clouds were beginning to break, giving way to a vibrant blue sky. The storm was over. Stacy sat up and looked down the beach. Pearl and Noah were with her. In the distance, she could see a ragged-looking Everest and Atlas and then, even farther down the beach, Ribsy and a bedraggled Paisley walking toward them. Stacy tried to stand, but her left knee buckled under her and she fell again to the sand. She looked down to see bright red blood running down her leg from a long gash right below her knee. Ribsy raced the last hundred yards or so over to her and knelt beside her. Stacy felt a strange sensation in her leg—the gash was closing! In a matter of seconds, the gash was healed, and the last few drops of blood trickled down Stacy's legs.

"Thank you, Ribsy," Stacy whispered. She knew how lucky she was to have found Ribsy and the other mesa wolves. *That gash could have easily become infected. The infection could have killed me.*

Stacy stood up and surveyed her surroundings. The island they had washed up on was . . . peculiar. It was covered in palm trees and tall, jagged mountains. Stacy felt a chill as a cool breeze blew through her wet hair.

"Breeze Island," she said aloud. "That's what we should call this place. But I don't think we should stay here too long."

Stacy looked at Everest and he nodded. *It's too windy on this island to camp here. It would be a constant struggle for Atlas to manage. And . . . I have a bad feeling about this place. I can't explain it. It's like . . . like people have died here.*

Stacy and the wolves climbed to the top of one of the mountains and, much to Stacy's delight, saw that Breeze Island was the largest in a small cluster of islands. To the south and east were two smaller islands, forming a trio. *Hopefully one of those will be more suitable for building a camp.*

The group quickly descended the mountain and swam over to the island to the east. Immediately, Stacy noticed this island wasn't as cold and windy. It wasn't mountainous either. It was flat and beautiful, with pristine white beaches and turquoise water. Stacy was just about to suggest they live here when she noticed something on the beach. A dozen or so tiny black dots were moving quickly across the sand. Stacy strode over to them and saw that they weren't black dots at all, but rather, baby sea turtles! Their shells were black, their heads were spotted—they were each only a couple inches long. *They must have just hatched!* Stacy watched the tiny turtles as they wriggled toward the water. Stacy noticed one of the turtles was lagging behind the others on the beach. He had a tiny bit of shell on his head, covering his eyes.

Stacy bent down and carefully peeled the bit of shell from the turtle's face. She yearned to pick the baby turtle up and help it down the beach to the ocean, but she knew that his struggle to the water was an essential part of his journey. He needed to fight his way down there to be strong enough to be able to swim. She also knew he was imprinting on his home beach, and that he would return here many times over the course of his long life. So instead, Stacy just crouched low to the ground and watched him in wonder as he determinedly shuffled through the white sand. Atlas kept the hungry gulls away, summoning a gust of wind anytime one of the birds swooped down too close.

I'm going to call you Hatch, Stacy thought.

"Well . . . I guess we can't live here either," Stacy said. "This is Hatch's Island."

She stood up and watched as Hatch made his way to the ocean.

"Good luck, little guy."

Stacy turned back to the group. With Breeze Island and Hatch's Island out of the running, there was only one island left. *We can't sail to any other islands . . . our boat is completely wrecked. I hope this next island is okay.*

Once more, Stacy dove into the ocean to swim to the next island. Noah swam beneath her, ready to lift Stacy up to the surface if she needed it. Everest was a good swimmer, but his massive frame kept him from being all that agile in the water. Paisley and Ribsy were the slowest. *They'll improve, though. It's not like they had a lot of opportunities to hone their swimming skills living in the dry mesa.* With Atlas and Pearl next to her, Stacy felt like she was one of the dolphins. She could stay underwater for as long as she wanted. Paisley had managed to save Stacy's satchel from the ship and, with it, the goggles she had tried to use with Molly. Stacy couldn't wait until they were settled on one of the islands and could go out for a proper swim where she could explore the ocean floor, collect shells, and get a closer look at the tropical fish who were all around her. But right now, she was determined to find a good home for the mesa pack. Stacy got lost in her thoughts as they swam. *Will they want to stay on this island? Will Paisley be able to grow enough food for them? Will they miss the diet they had back in the mesa? And how long will Everest, Noah, and I stay here to get them settled?*

Stacy and the others made their way onto the third island. It was the smallest of the three, but Stacy liked it almost instantly because it had a small inlet that came into the center of the island. *Pearl could use that to shelter for the night. She likes to spend more time in the water than out, after all.* Next to the inlet were two palm trees that had grown crookedly, forming an X shape. Stacy thought it could be a good place to build a shelter. As Stacy and the group walked from the center of the island to the opposite side from where they'd started, Paisley paid particularly close attention to the ground. Stacy imagined she was plotting out where to put a small garden and looking for a suitable patch of dirt in the center of the island where things could grow.

They reached the other side of the island quickly. To the west, Stacy could see the rocks the boat had crashed on. They walked on the beach to the island's southern tip, and Stacy's heart sank.

"Oh no . . ." she groaned. "What happened here?"

SIXTEEN

STACY LOOKED OUT over the beach at the dead mangrove trees. Their black and twisted roots were sticking out of the sand so far that the wolves could walk underneath them. Clumps of garbage had washed up on the shore and were strewn around the beach, along with the skeletons of several birds. Stacy looked beyond them into the water. *Oh no.* The coral reef near the shore looked to be dead as well. *What awful thing happened here?* Pearl and Noah swam out into the coral reef. Stacy followed after them. The coral was various shades of grays, browns, and white—not the vibrant colors Stacy knew it would be if it was healthy. *This beach is dying . . . but why?* Stacy had never seen coral before, but she knew that it was a living thing. And that it was a vital part of the ocean's ecosystem. Fish, turtles, dolphins, squid . . . they all relied on the coral—some ate the coral itself, and others ate the fish who fed on it. Stacy looked again at the dying coral before swimming back to shore. *We may have finally come across a rescue we cannot do. . . .*

Stacy, Pearl, and Noah rejoined the others on the island. Despite the dying beach, it seemed to Stacy that this island was the best spot for them to make a camp. Breeze Island was, well . . . too breezy. And besides that, it was the largest of the three islands and that meant that passing ships might be inclined to stop there and explore. *That was the island we crashed into, after all. We don't want that happening to someone else, and then they stumble onto a pack of magical wolves.* As for Hatch's Island, Stacy didn't want to do anything to disrupt the ecosystem there. *That island is the home beach of those turtles. I don't want them to return there to mate and get scared off by wolves.* This *is our little island. We should live here.* As Stacy was thinking, she noticed Paisley was standing near one of the dead mangrove trees, concentrating really hard on something. Stacy walked over to her and saw a small sprig of new growth on one of the mangrove's branches.

"Did you do that, Paisley?" Stacy asked, surprised. Paisley wagged her tail. "Well, that settles it then. We'll live here and Paisley and the rest of us can work on restoring the beach!"

The group walked back to the small lagoon in the center of the island and began to construct a shelter using the crossed palm trees. Stacy couldn't have been more pleased with her decision. She knew that if Paisley *was* able to regrow the mangrove trees, the greenery would provide excellent cover for the mesa pack from any explorers or passing boats. *They won't even be able to see the middle of the island!* She also knew the mangroves would protect against hurricanes and that their root systems would help stabilize the beach and restore the island. *It won't help the coral reef, but it's a start.*

Everest, Noah, and Atlas returned to the wreckage of their ship near Breeze Island and brought back with them some hardwood planks, rope, and what was left of the shredded sail. While they were gone, Paisley and Stacy worked to weave palm fronds together that Ribsy collected from around the island. Next, Stacy and Everest used the hardwood planks to create a crude treehouse where the two palm trees' trunks crossed. They laid the planks to form a platform about six or seven feet off the ground and then positioned the woven palm fronds on one side of the platform to make a lean-to. Stacy used the box of nails from the boat and a rock from the beach to hammer pieces of driftwood up the base of one of the palm trees, so she'd be able to climb up to the platform and down quickly.

Stacy looked up at the setting sun. She was tired from working so hard, but it felt good to have accomplished so much during their first day on the island. She walked over to the small lagoon near their campsite to wash up for dinner. Stacy had just stuck her hands into the water when she noticed a small fish swimming near her fingers. It was yellow and had large, wide eyes on either side of its small body. Its tiny mouth was turned up at the sides—making it look as if the fish was smiling.

"Aren't you cute?" Stacy said, extending her fingers to see if she could touch the fish in the water. Suddenly, the fish tripled in size.

"Ouch, ouch, ouch!" Stacy exclaimed.

The pufferfish had puffed out its spines in self-defense. Stacy yanked her hand out of the water and checked to see if the pufferfish poke had pierced her skin. Pufferfish are poisonous, but luckily, Stacy's skin hadn't been broken. *Phew! Not sure if Ribsy would have been able to heal me from that.*

Stacy turned away from the pufferfish, who she lovingly nicknamed Ouch, and looked back at the makeshift home she had built for the mesa pack. Atlas had jumped all the way to the top of the tallest of the two palms and was harvesting its coconuts. Everest was sitting on the plank platform they'd constructed, keeping an ever-watchful eye on what Stacy was doing. And Paisley was slung in the hammock Stacy had fashioned from the boat's ripped sail, napping peacefully—a tropical flower tucked behind one of her ears.

It was dusk now. Stacy reached into her satchel and pulled out the flint and steel Basil had given to her back in the taiga and used it to start a fire with kindling Ribsy had gathered earlier in the day. Noah had spent the rest of the afternoon fishing around the island. From the looks of his catch, he had taken care not to kill the same variety of fish twice. *That's good. We don't want to decimate any of the fish population while we're here.* Still, Stacy didn't like the idea of him fishing around the dying coral reef. *We should be looking for ways to increase life in the ocean here, not take life.* But she also knew that

Paisley needed time to grow food on the island. *Okay, we'll have a good meal tonight, and that should last the wolves for a while.* As for Stacy, she was loving all the new foods she'd been nibbling on that were growing naturally around the island. Coconut and coconut milk, bananas, and sugar apples—Stacy couldn't get enough of the sweet fruit.

After everyone ate dinner, Paisley returned to her cozy spot in the hammock while Pearl and Noah fell asleep near the lagoon. Ribsy set off to patrol the island for the night, while Everest turned around a couple times underneath the treehouse before plopping down on the sand. Stacy climbed up into the treehouse to sleep. It had been such a long day—from crashing their boat on the rocks, to exploring the three islands and building the treehouse. Stacy was already drifting off to sleep when Atlas jumped up and curled his soft body protectively around her.

Stacy woke up to the sweet smell of rice cooking in coconut milk with mango. *Wow, Paisley grew that already?* Stacy peered over the edge of the treehouse and watched Paisley as she toiled over the fire. Pearl and Noah were splashing around in the lagoon. Everest was now by Stacy's side, dozing.

"Wake up, Everest!" Stacy said, gently nudging the

giant wolf. "Paisley's made breakfast!"

Despite eating a big meal the night before, Stacy was ravenous. As she tucked into the mango and rice, she couldn't help but think about Page, Molly, her cats, and the other wolves and wishing they were all here with her on the island. *Addison would get along so well with Paisley. She would love getting to create new dishes with the food Paisley can grow. And Milquetoast and Pipsqueak would be in heaven with all the varieties of tropical fish they'd be eating here. Tucker and Ribsy would probably get along too—their powers are so similar.* Stacy was so lost in thought and savoring the deliciousness of her breakfast that it took her a long time to recognize Milo the bat fluttering in the air in front of her.

"Milo!"

Stacy was ecstatic to see the little brown bat. Partly because she had come to love the adorable creature, but mostly because she knew his presence here meant that Wink and Basil had returned to the taiga safely with Page and Molly. *I can't believe you flew so far!* Stacy had assumed Milo would hand off his message to other bats who could locate Stacy, but she realized that he must have deemed this information too important to not deliver himself. Stacy was so relieved they were okay.

"Welcome to our little island, Milo," Stacy said,

putting a few morsels of mango on a nearby piece of driftwood for Milo to munch on. "You're welcome to stay with us as long as you'd like."

After eating her fill of mango and coconut rice, Stacy walked with Milo and Everest to the beach at the north side of the little island. Ribsy, Noah, and Atlas were standing near the water where Pearl was swimming, everyone looking slightly distressed. *Oh no. What's the matter now? Is everyone feeling okay?* Everest ran to the pack and then turned to Stacy and scrawled a set of runes in the sand. Stacy was surprised he'd learned the language already (and that she could read it)— apparently she'd translated enough of the diary that she was becoming fluent.

"R-E-S-C-U-E," Stacy said with a gasp, suddenly realizing why everyone looked so anxious. "Oh my . . . we have our first ocean rescue!"

SEVENTEEN

STACY IMMEDIATELY NOTICED the look of concern in Everest's silver eyes. And she knew exactly what he was thinking. *I haven't proven to him that I can do a rescue in the ocean. My first attempt to rescue an animal in the ocean ended up being just a floating pile of trash and then Noah and Pearl had to rescue me. And then there was the boat crash . . . that didn't exactly end well either.* Stacy stared into Everest's eyes. *Please let me do this. Noah and Pearl will be with me the entire time. And Atlas too! They'll keep me safe.* Stacy expected the alpha wolf to shake his head no. After all, this would be the first rescue where he wouldn't be able to be there in case Stacy needed saving. He would have to put all his trust in Noah and two mesa wolves he'd known for less than a week. *Remember, you'll be able to hear my thoughts the entire time. It will be like you're there with me.* Everest looked down at the sand, mulling over his decision. Finally, he looked up, exchanged a glance with Atlas, and then turned back to Stacy and gave a short nod. *Yes!* Stacy rushed over to embrace him. *I promise I'll be careful, boy. I promise.*

Noah ran to fetch the goggles from Stacy's satchel back at the treehouse while Stacy tied her hair back with a piece of seaweed and waded into the water toward Pearl, who was facing north toward Breeze Island.

"You must have gone swimming pretty far this morning, huh?" Stacy said to Pearl right before dipping her entire body underwater and getting her hair wet. Noah returned with her goggles, which Stacy promptly put on. He also brought the emergency flare, which Stacy tucked into the pocket of her cutoff shorts. Before Stacy could say anything else, Pearl took off swimming.

"Everest, bring Ribsy to Breeze Island," Stacy said. "Who knows—we may end up needing his ability. All right, Pearl . . . lead the way!"

Stacy swam over to Noah and climbed onto his

back, clasping her hands around his large neck. Atlas positioned himself on Noah's right side and the three wolves began swimming. At first, Noah glided along the surface of the ocean so Stacy could keep her head above water. But as they approached Breeze Island, Pearl swerved east and Noah suddenly dove deep underwater to keep up with her.

Noah descended deeper and deeper. Atlas was nearby, allowing Stacy to breathe. She took a breath of air and looked around her. The color of the water had changed from bright turquoise to a brilliant dark blue. *We're in the deep ocean now!* The wolves swam through a large school of tropical fish in a kaleidoscope of different colors. Stacy looked above her and saw a large sea turtle and then gasped as she peered below her at a massive whale with a calf. *Everest, I wish you could see this. There's a whole other world down here!*

Stacy looked up and realized that Pearl had swum in between Breeze Island and Hatch's Island and was diving even deeper now, toward the sea floor. Suddenly, their destination came into view . . . a sunken ship! Stacy could only imagine what Everest was thinking right now—a sunken ship was probably a little more dangerous than he was expecting. Stacy looked at the massive ship as Noah dove closer. Stacy guessed it was at least a hundred years old. It had a giant mast and a lookout—Stacy knew those were called crow's nests. Both were now covered in algae. The ship's massive wooden hull had barnacles growing all over it and several giant, gaping holes. *Is there an animal in there?* Stacy took another big breath from Atlas's air bubble and tried to mentally prepare herself for the rescue. Pearl brought them around to the back of the shipwreck to a tiny rusted porthole—much smaller than the one that had been in their boat and too small for any of her wolves to fit through. *Pearl wants me to go in there?* Stacy swam up to the porthole and stared into the darkness inside the ship. She wasn't sure she could even fit through the porthole herself, but if there was an animal inside who needed help, she was willing to give it a try.

Stacy wriggled her way through the porthole. It was a tight squeeze, but her shoulders just fit. She swam all the way inside and then immediately turned back to the porthole, grabbing the bottom rim of it to keep herself from floating away. Atlas was staring back at her. Stacy leaned into the porthole to discover he'd created an air bubble. *Brilliant! I can swim back here whenever I need to take a breath.* Stacy had to admit, it was less than ideal to be separated from the wolves on the other side of the porthole. She didn't even know what animal they were rescuing yet. *Guess I'd better have a look around. It's so dark though.* A thought occurred to her. She took the emergency flare from her pocket and brought it up to the air bubble in the porthole. She twisted the top off to reveal a small fire striker on the flare's cap. She put it to the other side and pulled it hard across the top of the flare. A red flame sputtered to life, and then burned brightly. Atlas looked at Stacy, amazed. Stacy turned away from the wolf, not sure if what she was about to do would work. She plunged the flare into the water . . . it didn't extinguish! It was getting all of the oxygen it needed to burn from a chemical stored inside it—no air necessary! *Wow. Basil would love this. Okay, here goes nothing.* Stacy pushed off from the porthole into the darkness, holding the flare out in front of her. The room she was in was small—probably twenty feet wide and fifteen feet long. There was a wall of windows along the back of the room, which were still intact. And on the opposite side, a door with a heavy lock on it. *Oh, that's why Pearl couldn't find another way in besides the porthole.* The room was filled with furniture that had obviously shifted around from its original location. There was a large wooden desk with a rolltop cover, an impressive chair turned on its side and covered in kelp, and a toppled-over bookcase with soggy tomes scattered around the wood plank floor. Stacy swam down into the small space between the tipped-over bookcase and the desk and found a gilded locker—a treasure chest?! *This must have been the ship captain's quarters.* Stacy swam back to Atlas for a breath. She wasn't sure how much longer the flare would last, and she still hadn't found the animal who needed rescuing. Even with the flare, the room was just too dark and cluttered. There could be a dozen or more animals in the room with Stacy and she wouldn't have known—there were too many good places to hide. Suddenly, Stacy noticed a flicker of movement near the ceiling of the captain's room. She took a deep breath in and swam up, the red flare instantly illuminating the animal who needed help.

Stacy couldn't believe what she was looking at. A baby dolphin was floating near the room's ceiling . . . its nose stuck in what looked to be an old empty bottle. *It must have swum in here through the porthole and now it can't get out.* Fortunately, the bottle was not covering its tiny blowhole and there was a small pocket of air in the corner of the room, which was keeping the dolphin alive. Stacy had read about bottlenose dolphins and had even heard of a ship in a bottle before, but nothing could have prepared her for a bottlenose dolphin in a ship with its nose in a bottle.

Suddenly, the baby dolphin began frantically swimming around, thrashing its body from side to side, desperately trying to separate itself from the bottle. It swam toward the porthole but the bottle clanged on the side of it, knocking the dolphin backward. *Poor thing! It must be so scared.*

Stacy's flare fizzled out, but her eyes had adjusted to the darkness around her. She knew there was no time to lose. The dolphin calf was exhausted and needed to be back with its mother. Stacy dropped the flare and reached her arms out, trying to grasp the dolphin in her hands. It took several minutes, with Stacy returning every thirty seconds to the porthole to catch her breath before attempting to capture the dolphin again. Eventually, the dolphin tired and slowed down, giving Stacy the perfect opportunity to wrap her hands around the bottle. Holding the calf out in front of her by the end of the glass bottle, Stacy pulled as hard as she could as a dark shadow passed behind her—*Yes! Got it!*

Stacy pulled the newly freed baby dolphin into her arms and swam to the porthole. Stacy took a breath first, and then pushed the dolphin through the porthole to where Pearl was waiting—presumably to bring the dolphin back to its mother. Stacy was about to swim out of the cabin too, but then she remembered the treasure chest. *I wonder . . .* Stacy took another breath and then dove down toward the chest. She expected it to be locked, so it came as a big surprise to her when it popped open the second her fingers touched the rusted latch.

Stacy's eyes widened in awe. Inside the chest was a beautiful tiara, bejeweled with emeralds. As she reached into the chest to take it, a cold tentacle brushed against her arm.

Stacy grabbed the tiara and spun around into a cloud of black squid ink. *BLECCCKK! Help!* Stacy wiped the ink off her goggles and swam as fast as she could to the porthole. Her mouth was full of the ink and she could feel it beginning to seep through her goggles. She stuck her head into the space of air in the porthole and pulled her goggles off and spit the ink out. Noah and Atlas treaded water beside the ship, concerned.

"BLUH, BLEH, UGHH," Stacy spewed. The ink was all over her clothes and in her hair. "That squid was obviously just as scared of me as I was of it. Get me out of here."

Stacy reached for Noah and he pulled her out of the porthole. Together with Atlas, they raced Stacy up to the surface and back to Breeze Island, where Everest was waiting rather impatiently for them, along with Ribsy and Paisley. As they paddled to the shore, Stacy looked back in the direction of the ship and saw Pearl swimming with a pod of dolphins, including the calf and its mother—reunited. *Thank goodness Pearl found the dolphin when she did. That had to be one of the craziest rescues yet.* Stacy staggered out of the water holding her goggles in one hand and the jeweled tiara in the other. She looked at Everest, held up the tiara, and smiled.

"At least I got a reward!"

EIGHTEEN

STACY LIT A fire with her flint and steel. It was the next morning and, after several dips in the lagoon, Stacy had finally washed all the cephalopod ink from her hair. It was the first gloomy day the pack had seen since arriving on the island and, after such an action-packed day yesterday, Stacy decided she would rest all day while the wolves continued to work on their various projects. She had a simple but delicious breakfast of bananas, rice, cassava root, and coconut milk and then settled into the hammock underneath the palm trees. Stacy was resolved that today was the day she would finally decode the rest of the tundra explorer's journal. She was determined to finish the translation and read the journal in its entirety—something she was almost able to do now without needing to check the key.

> *Today is a dark day. We returned to the tundra to discover that Diamond went into labor earlier than we anticipated. She is dead. Two pups are also dead, but one survived. Somehow. Ames is missing. We suspect he left when things took a turn for the worse during the birthing, hoping to find us. I cannot fully express the pain of discovering such a grisly scene in a place that has also brought me so much joy over the last decade. We will continue looking for Ames and introduce the surviving pup to the taiga pack in a few weeks when he is stable and can eat meat. His eyes are open already. They are a beautiful rust brown. We've named him Garnet.*

Oh, Wink. A tear rolled down Stacy's cheek. She brushed it away. Everest, who was lying next to Stacy in the hammock, buried his head in the fabric. *Wink survived because that's his ability. Just like Basil was fast as a pup and Addison was so smart she picked up some of the rune language—the wolves' future powers were present even from birth. That's why Wink lived. That's why Wink was younger than the rest of the pack when I came to live with them in the taiga. That's why Diamond's name was crossed out in the rune along with the two numbers next to Garnet. And the "Where are you" was a message from the tundra explorer to Ames. He was searching the tundra for help. He never found it. He would have returned to see the names scratched out. Poor Ames! He was left all alone in the ice cavern, waiting for the explorer to return. He carved "Here now" into the ice and continued to look for the explorer. He used what little strength he had left to carve runes out on the tundra that Addison found, hoping to be reunited with his family.* Stacy turned the last page of the journal and read the final entry.

We're back in the tundra after introducing Garnet to the taiga litter. The introduction went well. Ames is still not here. I am very concerned that something has happened to him. I'm going to leave this journal here, seeing as I have filled it. I will buy another one the next time I am in the village for supplies. One piece of good news is that the art my partner produced while living in the Arctic with me has been well received by the public. So much so that it has afforded us a helicopter that will make trips to the tundra and taiga much easier. Our daughter is getting old enough that we want to start bringing her along with us as well. Our first trip with her will be to the taiga to check up on Garnet's progress. After that, we will launch a larger search effort for Ames. Beyond that—we've heard of a sighting of a pair of white wolves with four pups in the southern mesa biome. We may use the helicopter to investigate. If there are more wolves of this kind in the mesa, we hope to find them before hunters do. Until then, good-bye.

NINETEEN

STACY SAT IN the hammock in shock. *A helicopter? Our daughter? A trip to the taiga? The tundra explorer . . . she was my mother.* Everest nuzzled Stacy's shoulder. Stacy felt like she was losing her parents all over again. She'd hoped to someday meet the explorer. Learn from her. Now that would never happen. She was dead. *And my father was the artist. We were all in the helicopter together—but only I survived. They never made it to the mesa biome. The mesa pack . . . hunters must have killed their parents. And I am the only person in the world who knows about these wolves.* The weight of this thought pushed down on Stacy's shoulders. *It's up to me. To protect* *them . . . it's up to me.* Stacy was devastated, but a small part of her was also so proud to be the daughter of such an amazing woman. Caring for the wolves—the way she had been for years—was carrying on her parents' legacy. Everything she'd gone through—the expedition on the tundra, coming back to the mesa, and helping Pearl—it was what needed to be done.

I've got to get back to the taiga and tell Addison all of this. As much as Stacy loved island life, she knew they would need to leave soon so she could tell the rest of the pack what she'd learned from the journal . . . and so she could pay what she owed for Pip's visit to the animal hospital. *Pip! I'd forgotten about him for a minute. Pip and Milquetoast and Page and Molly . . . they're my responsibility to take care of. But . . . will the mesa wolves come with us? They seem to like it here, but will they be okay on their own?*

Suddenly, Paisley came running toward Stacy and Everest, beckoning them to follow her.

"What is it, Pais?" Stacy said, scrambling out of the hammock. They followed Paisley to the dead beach. Stacy stopped running and bent over to catch her breath. When she looked up, she couldn't believe what she was looking at. . . .

TWENTY

STACY GAZED OUT over the ocean at the thriving coral reef. The water was teeming with tropical fish swimming among the vibrant blues, pinks, yellows, and reds of the reef. *Paisley did it! She restored the coral!* The mangrove forest was flourishing, and Paisley had even begun growing a protective wall of palm trees and shrubs to create a barrier around the entire island to hide. *They'll be safe here; everyone will think this island is overgrown. They'll have no idea about the tropical paradise inside.* Everest appeared alongside Stacy, holding her swimming goggles so that Stacy could get a better view of the revitalized section of the ocean.

"Thank you, Everest," Stacy said to him. Then she put on the goggles and dove into the warm water to inspect the coral with Paisley and Pearl.

Stacy couldn't believe how much the reef had changed during the short time she had been on the island. It was so beautiful and lush—like an underwater forest. She saw animals everywhere she looked. There were sea horses and little orange-and-white-striped clown fish. She even saw Ouch the pufferfish and Hatch, the baby sea turtle, who had practically doubled in size since the last time she saw him. There were yellow sponges, crabs, and starfish too. And the dolphins were there! Stacy could see that the revitalization of the coral reef had strengthened the ocean's food web. Everyone would be able to eat and survive now that Paisley had rehabilitated the coral. She'd literally saved hundreds of animals in an area that had likely taken hundreds of thousands (if not millions) of years to form.

Stacy came up for air and turned on her back to float. Obviously, the reef still had a way to go to be completely healed, to have the chance to expand and grow. But with Paisley here, there was no question in Stacy's mind that it would happen. *Paisley will see to it.* Stacy thought about the mesa pack as she swam to the shore and sat down on the sand to wait for the sun to dry her off. *The mesa wolves fit in perfectly here. Obviously Pearl needs to be here and can swim all around the islands to see if any animals need rescuing . . . the sea turtles like Hatch, dolphins like the one from the shipwreck, whales, fish, squid, sharks, jellyfish . . . she can bring them to Ribsy, who can heal them. Atlas can keep watch for passing ships and protect the birds—seagulls, hummingbirds, plovers, and pelicans—who live here. And Paisley's talent is with the island vegetation. Making sure all the plants and trees and coral and kelp are sustained. She can maintain the reef and take care of any litter that washes up on the shore. They'll keep this part of the world safe—just like my pack does back in the taiga. They're the sentinels of this ocean!*

Everest walked over and sat next to Stacy. Stacy looked to him and he nodded. *He agrees with me.* They looked out at Pearl, Ribsy, Atlas, and Paisley all playing together in the surf. *They belong here. They've found their mission.*

It occurred to Stacy that she'd found her mission as well. Without the Arctic explorer . . . *my mother* . . . around to study and protect the wolves with abilities, this was Stacy's secret to keep now. Her wolf pack would continue to protect the animals and nature around them in the taiga. And the mesa pack, now permanently relocated to the ocean, would protect the environment here. *Who knows! Maybe I'll find other wolves in the future in different parts of the world—I could create a rescue network of the wolves, living in secrecy and guarding the planet!*

Stacy knew what she needed to do. She decided right then and there that she would return to the taiga as soon as she could and prepare to start school in the fall. *Reading every book I can get my hands on and picking up things here and there from Addison and my other wolves just isn't enough. If I'm going to do this, I need to get as much education as I can so I'll know what to do in any situation I'm faced with.* Stacy was confident she'd be able to go to school in the village and still sneak back to the taiga to live with her pack and go on rescue missions. *It's perfect. And who knows, maybe I'll even go to Village State University one day.*

For the next several days, Everest, Noah, and Atlas worked on salvaging more planks from the boat wreckage to use for constructing a raft. Stacy helped as well, once again using a stone and the box of nails to fortify the raft. Leftover rope from the boat's sails was used to fashion two harnesses for Noah and Pearl to pull the raft back to the rocky beach where their ocean adventure had started. The plan was for Pearl to accompany them at least that far, and then she'd return to what Stacy had named Our Little Island while Stacy, Noah, and Everest journeyed on to the taiga.

And just like that, before Stacy was ready at all, the raft was finished and it was time to say good-bye. Leaving at sunset meant that they would make it back to the beach on the mainland under the cover of night. The water was still and smooth, and they'd be able to make camp in the cave they'd spent so many nights in while they were restoring the boat. And then the next morning Stacy, Noah, and Everest could get an early start back to the taiga.

Stacy stood on the beach with Everest on the raft and Noah and Pearl in the water. Paisley was the first wolf to come over to Stacy for a good-bye. Paisley had something in her mouth—the bandanna that Stacy had given to her the first day they met. She had used some natural pigments from around the island to dye it a beautiful shade of light blue, Stacy's favorite color. Stacy took the bandanna from Paisley and used it to wipe away the tears that were running down her cheeks. Then she threw her arms around the wolf.

"I love you, Paisley," Stacy whispered. "I'll come back to visit you as soon as I can." Stacy knew that in all likelihood that probably wouldn't be until it was winter in the taiga, but she couldn't bear the thought that she was saying good-bye to Paisley for that many months.

Ribsy was next.

"You saved Pearl's life, you know that, right?" Stacy said, giving Ribsy a big hug. "She's lucky to have you. We all are." Ribsy bowed his head to Stacy and Everest.

Stacy was dreading saying good-bye to Atlas the most. He had been the hardest wolf to befriend by far, but now that he had warmed up to Stacy (and saved her life several times), they had bonded. It was like Stacy was leaving a small piece of her heart behind on the island with him.

"I love you too, Atlas," Stacy sobbed into the wolf's soft coat.

Before she could change her mind, Stacy let go of Atlas and jumped onto the raft with Everest.

"I'll see you soon," Stacy said, choking back more tears. Noah and Pearl began to pull the raft forward toward the setting sun. Milo the bat fluttered at Stacy's shoulder while Stacy clung to Everest. She looked back at Our Little Island as it became smaller and smaller and she could no longer see Paisley, Ribsy, and Atlas standing on the beach. As the island disappeared into the distance, she heard a sorrowful howl from Atlas. Stacy wiped the tears from her eyes again with her bandanna and then dug her hands into Everest's thick fur.

I miss them already.

Stacy couldn't help but be amazed at how much her

life had changed over the last few weeks. She hadn't known the wolves from the mesa then—she hadn't even known they existed. And now they were part of her family. She looked at Pearl, who was pulling the raft with ease in the water; Noah struggling to keep up. Stacy closed her eyes and enjoyed her last moments in the deep ocean, knowing her life was about to change even more.

EPILOGUE

STACY COULD BARELY see where she was going over the tall stack of books she was carrying home to her cave in the taiga. It was September now and, despite all her worrying, Stacy's first day of school in the village could not have gone better. Addison and Everest had walked her to the school in the morning—Everest camouflaged himself and Addison as they neared the schoolhouse. Addison gave her a packed lunch and her pair of drugstore reading glasses for Stacy to borrow. Stacy gave Addison the biggest hug good-bye before nervously entering the building. But all of Stacy's fretting had been for nothing. Her teacher was patient and easy to understand, her classmates were kind and welcoming, and not once did Stacy feel as if she was too dumb to be in the class she was. In fact, she could remember at least five times during the day when she had raised her hand to answer a question the teacher asked—and had answered correctly! Now she was heading home and she couldn't be more excited to tell Addison all about how the day had gone and what she had learned.

Stacy and the wolves had experienced a very uneventful summer, which, after everything that had happened over the last year, was perfectly fine with her. She had spent most of the summer volunteering at the Village County Animal Shelter and planting saplings around the taiga to regrow areas the villagers demolished the previous summer. She also finished working off Pipsqueak's veterinary bill by assisting Dr. Kay at the animal hospital and even made a little bit of extra money washing dishes for Miriam at the diner. She'd stashed away some of the money she earned in the tin on her bookshelf in case one of her animals had another emergency that required a trip to the vet. The rest of the money she spent on a few new outfits to wear to school; some school supplies; and collars for Page, Molly, Milquetoast, and Pipsqueak. Lastly, she purchased a new journal to replace her old one that she had completely filled with stories of everything that had transpired over the last year—everything from animal rescues in the taiga, Page's rescue, the timber wolf pack and the forest fire, her pack's first trip to the mesa, Molly's rescue, their expedition on the tundra and—most recently—their adventure with the mesa pack to the beach and their transformation into the sentinels in the deep ocean.

Speaking of transformations, the cave that Stacy, her pets, and her wolves called home in the taiga had undergone a bit of a transformation as well. Addison, Tucker, Wink, and Basil had surprised Stacy while she was away and had expanded the cave. They were likely preparing for a scenario in which Stacy brought the mesa pack home to live with them if the tropical island had proved uninhabitable, however their improvements were still much appreciated considering Stacy now had four pets living in the cave. First, Basil had created a small chamber near the cave's hearth for proper chest storage—a place where they could keep extra food and supplies, including lots of firewood for the cold months in the taiga. Meanwhile, Tucker, Wink, and Addison had dug out the back wall of the cave, expanding the room significantly. Next to the cave's small spring of water, Tucker and Wink had dragged in a fallen birch tree and propped it up as a perfect makeshift cat tower for Milquetoast and Pipsqueak to play and nap on. And opposite that area, Addison had expanded Stacy's bookshelf—giving Stacy additional space to spread out her homework and keep the growing collection of books she was borrowing from the village library. Part of Miriam registering Stacy for school in August had meant

Stacy getting her own library card. Stacy could check out science books on whatever topics she wanted. And that's just what she'd done.

As she approached the clearing near the cave, Stacy stepped in a patch of soft podzol and lost her footing—the stack of books in her arms swaying back and forth. They were just on the verge of toppling over when suddenly a large tail appeared, steadying the books before they crashed down around Stacy.

"Thanks, Everest," Stacy said. "That would have been disastrous."

Stacy and Everest walked into the cave where Addison and Noah were busy canning cat food to keep in the pantry for the winter. Noah was having a hard time keeping up with Pipsqueak's appetite, so they were trying to get a supply saved so he didn't have to fish every day. It had been a pretty big shock for Stacy when she had arrived home with Noah and Everest to find that Pipsqueak was no longer a scrawny kitten, but a giant fluffy cat twice the size of Milquetoast. Stacy smiled lovingly at Addison and Noah and then stepped over Wink and Tucker, who were sleeping in front of the fire, on her way to set her books down at her desk. Basil had already left for the night to start her shift of patrol duty on the ridge above their cave. Next, Stacy walked over to see Milquetoast and Pipsqueak, who were hanging out on their birch tree cat tower. Stacy picked Pipsqueak up—she needed both her arms to hold him now. He purred loudly. Milquetoast hopped down from the highest perch on the birch tree and climbed onto Stacy's shoulders while Page and Molly ran over to greet Stacy.

Stacy walked back over to her desk and sat down to begin writing in her new journal. She took a fresh pen out of her box of school supplies and began to write in her mother's language, in which she was now fluent.

My name is Stacy. If you are reading this, then you have also discovered the secret I discovered—and that my mother first discovered—of a new wolf species. I implore you to keep this secret and join me in my fight to protect them and use their powers for good in the world. I have no doubt that the wolves you are with have changed your life, the way my life was forever changed by Everest, Basil, Addison, Noah, Tucker,

Wink, Atlas, Ribsy, Paisley, and Pearl.
They've given me a purpose and a love for
the natural planet and the animals in it.
They've given me a family of pets to care for
and who care for me. I don't know where I
will be when you are reading this, as I expect
my work with the wolves to take me on many
adventures all over the world. But I hope you
will join me. Join me in being a guardian
of the forest and a sentinel of the ocean. Join
me . . . in being a wild rescuer.

THE END.

STACY'S FAVORITE WORDS FROM THE BOOK

arduous—tiring and challenging. Example: *Translating the runes in the journal was a slow and arduous task.*

arroyo—a ravine formed by fast, flowing water (possibly after a rainstorm) in a dry biome. Example: *Basil slowed down to cross a dry arroyo in the mesa.*

bristled—specifically related to an animal's hair or fur moving as a result of anxiousness or anger. Example: *Everest bristled at Stacy's suggestion.*

cephalopod—a predatory mollusk, like a squid or an octopus. Example: *After several dips in the lagoon, Stacy had finally washed all the cephalopod ink from her hair.*

chagrin—annoyance or disappointment. Example: *Milquetoast and Pipsqueak made noise around the cave all night long . . . much to Everest's chagrin.*

clambered—moved or climbed in an awkward manner, perhaps using your hands and feet at the same time. Example: *Stacy and her pack clambered over the rocky shore to get closer to the cave.*

concoction—a mixture, possibly strange, of ingredients. Example: *Paisley stirred the sticky concoction with a branch.*

confabbed—had a private conversation with someone. Example: *Everest confabbed with Atlas and walked over to the firepit.*

decimate—destroy all or a large part of something. Example: *Stacy didn't want Noah's fishing to decimate any of the local fish population.*

dilapidated—in a state of ruin, usually from age or lack of care. Example: *Poking out of the sea cave, just far enough for Stacy to spot it, was a dilapidated sailboat.*

disheveled—looking untidy in appearance. Example: *The disheveled wolf had little bits of twigs and sage sticking out from her fur.*

disposition—someone's personality or character. Example: *Stacy knew wolves didn't really smile, but Tucker's cheery disposition made it seem like he was.*

epiphany—a major realization or discovery. Example: *A few days had passed since Stacy's epiphany about the possible existence of a mesa wolf pack.*

fortnight—two weeks. Often confused with a video game that Stacy will never play. Example: *Stacy planned on staying in the mesa for a fortnight.*

furrow—to wrinkle your forehead or face. Example: *The farmer lowered his rifle and furrowed his brow.*

gallivanting—traveling or roaming about for fun. Example: *Basil decided to help Noah with his fishing while Wink was off gallivanting somewhere.*

gilded—covered or coated in gold. Example: *Stacy swam down and found a gilded locker—a treasure chest?!*

gnawed—chewed or nibbled on persistently. Example: *Stacy played fetch with Page for a long time while Molly gnawed on seaweed pods.*

grisly—gruesome and causing horror. Example: *I cannot fully express the pain of discovering such a grisly scene in a place that has also brought me so much joy over the last decade.*

implore—ask with urgency or beg someone to do something. Example: *I implore you to keep this secret and join me in my fight to protect them and use their powers for good in the world.*

inconsolable—in a state of sadness or grief and unable to be comforted. Example: *The elder wolf had passed away, leaving Tucker weakened and inconsolable.*

insatiable—unable to be satisfied or quenched. Example: *Pipsqueak's appetite was insatiable.*

leery—cautious or suspicious. Example: *Molly was leery of the ocean.*

metamorphic—a rock that has been transformed by natural causes such as pressure or heat. Example: *Stacy knew lapis lazuli was a metamorphic rock.*

morsel—a small amount of food. Example: *Stacy put a few morsels of mango on a nearby piece of driftwood for Milo to munch on.*

penchant—a liking or habit of doing something. Example: *Basil had super speed and a penchant for pyrotechnics.*

scree—the mound of loose rocks and pebbles that forms at the base of a steep mountain. Example: *The seven of them traversed the rocky scree at the bottom of the mesa where the abandoned mineshaft was located.*

sentinel—someone whose job it is to keep watch. Example: *Atlas, Ribsy, Paisley, and Pearl are the sentinels in the deep ocean.*

subcutaneous—situated or applied under the skin. Example: *The doctor gave Pipsqueak subcutaneous fluids.*

teeming—to be very full of (or swarming with) something. Example: *The water was teeming with tropical fish swimming among the vibrant blues, pinks, yellows, and reds of the reef.*

tome—a long and heavy book. Example: *There was a large wooden desk and a toppled-over bookcase with soggy tomes scattered around the wood plank floor.*

topography—a detailed depiction or drawing of an area's geographical features. Example: *She instantly recognized that the map's topography was of this region.*

tutelage—the teaching or instruction someone gives you. Example: *Stacy had grown up under the tutelage of a super-smart wolf, Addison.*

volition—free will; the act of making your own decision. Example: *Every other time she and her wolves had left the taiga, it had not been of their own volition.*

zagged—to take a sharp turn. Example: *Basil looked up and zagged in the direction Stacy had pointed.*

MEET THE REAL-LIFE PIPSQUEAK!

When Pip was adopted by Stacy, he weighed only two and a half pounds at twelve weeks of age. He was diagnosed with feline infectious peritonitis—a usually fatal condition that can affect kittens. Stacy sought a second opinion from a specialist who recommended she quarantine Pip away from Milquetoast and monitor his progress. After several weeks . . . Pip got better! Stacy chronicled the highs and lows of Pip's health journey on her YouTube channel youtube.com/StacyVlogs.

Breed: unknown mix . . . something big though!

Age: 3 years old

Rescue date: January 26, 2018

Favorite activity: terrorizing his older brother, Milquetoast

Favorite foods: any kind of fish

Fun fact: Pipsqueak really does squeak! At first, his meows were completely silent. Now he makes a small squeak when he meows. So even though he's grown into a huge cat, his name still suits him!

GET TO KNOW A SEA TURTLE SCIENTIST!

The animals and situations in *Wild Rescuers: Sentinels in the Deep Ocean* are purely fictional. To learn about the real creatures of the oceans, Stacy interviewed a marine biologist!

Name:
Nathan J. Robinson, PhD

Current job:
Researcher at the Fundación Oceanogràfic in Valencia, Spain

Which oceans have you conducted research in?
I have been lucky enough to work in the Atlantic, Pacific, and Indian Oceans. I have also worked in several smaller seas including the Gulf of Mexico, the Mediterranean, and the Caribbean. I feel very privileged to have been able to travel to so many incredible places as part of my job, and it is a definite perk of being a marine biologist. I have even had the opportunity to go places that no one has ever gone before. For example, I traveled below a depth of 1,000 m (3,280 ft) in a submarine to explore the bottom of the Caribbean Sea!

Dr. Robinson and the Bahamian minister of education in an OceanX submarine heading into the deep waters off the Bahamas.

Is it true you captured footage of a giant squid?

I am immensely proud to say that this is true! In the summer of 2019, Dr. Edith Widder and I recorded the first-ever footage of a live giant squid in US waters. This was the second time that this species has ever been caught alive on camera in the world, and it was a huge achievement in the field of deep-sea exploration. I still find it incredible that this deep-sea giant, which can grow to a size of over 14 m (46 ft) and was the inspiration for the legendary "Kraken," was able to avoid being caught on camera for so long!

Dr. Robinson and Dr. Edith Widder standing next to the camera they used to record the giant squid.

What is one thing you want everyone to know about sea turtles?

Many people know that sea turtles are endangered, but I would like everyone to know that whoever they are and wherever they live, they can do something to help protect sea turtles around the world. One of the biggest threats to sea turtles today is marine plastic pollution, as sea turtles often confuse plastic objects for food. For example, floating plastic bags can be easily confused for jellyfish, a favorite meal of most sea turtles. If you want to help sea turtles, it is as simple as remembering to refuse, reduce, reuse, or recycle any single-use plastics in your life so they do not end up in the oceans!

What should you do if you find baby sea turtles on the beach?

If you ever find a baby sea turtle, it is important not to pick it up. Instead, you should try to contact any local authorities or organizations that work in sea turtle conservation. They will be able to provide direct advice and can likely send a team to help. However, if you do not know who to contact, then the best advice is to stay behind the turtle to not block its view of the ocean, otherwise it will not know which way to crawl. You can also use your body and any other object to create shade for the turtle. During the day, the sand can be dangerously hot for a hatchling.

What is a TurtleCam?

A TurtleCam is a device we built to discover more about the secret lives of turtles. Essentially, it is like a head-mounted GoPro but for a sea turtle. With these devices, we can get a first-person (or should it be first-turtle?) perspective on how these animals see the world around them. These TurtleCams are helping us learn more about what sea turtles eat, where they live, and what threats they face. We are even getting information on how turtles interact with each other—in other words, we are studying their social lives!

What should young people do if they are interested in ocean conservation?

My biggest recommendation for any young people interested in getting involved in ocean conservation is to volunteer. There are countless organizations working in ocean conservation worldwide, and they need your help! So do your research, find out which volunteer organizations are working in the areas that interest you the most, and get in contact.

About Nathan Robinson:

Nathan Robinson is a marine biologist and science communicator. His research focuses on using new technologies to answer important ecological questions while simultaneously raising awareness about the threats facing our oceans. Nathan first began following this career path after a video of him removing a plastic straw from a sea turtle's nose helped ignite a global movement to combat plastic pollution in our oceans. He has since moved to several other exciting projects, including using animal-borne cameras to investigate the secret lives of sea turtles and capturing the first-ever footage of a giant squid in US waters. He hopes that his work will help engage global audiences in marine science and provide the impetus we need to keep protecting our ocean planet.

You can follow his work online.

ACKNOWLEDGMENTS

To my wonderful readers—the enthusiastic ones I've had the privilege of meeting on my book tours and the ones I interact with on social media—I don't know what I ever did to deserve your immense love and support. Thank you.

Thank you to my mom and dad. Thank you to Vivienne To and Jessie Gang, who were with me through this entire journey. It has been such a pleasure working with you both over the years. Thank you to my editor, David Linker, my copyeditor, Christina MacDonald, and to Alison Klapthor, Alexandra Rakaczki, and all the fantastic folks at HarperCollins I've gotten to work with on this series. I owe a tremendous amount of gratitude to Maddie Lansbury, who not only provided the runes again for this book, but also helped me close way too many plot holes I created in the first book when I didn't quite know what the series was going to turn into. Thank you to the best Twitch mods in the universe, UrsulasRevenge and GalacticMermaidAdventures. I also want to thank one of my intrepid readers, Evan, who guessed where this book was headed and gave me some inspiration as well! And to my incomparable Papa Ford, who passed away last year at age 100—I wish you had been able to read the last book in the series.

I would also like to thank my generous pawtrons from patreon.com/StacyPlays—your support means the world to me, thank you: Adrien W., Ali S., Anhmye T., Austin A., Bree C., Brian C., Carl C. & Family, Carson F., Charlotte S., Chris H., Cierra D., Claudia R., Curtis H., Dan M., Devin C., Dez W., Emily L., Emily W., Erika D., Eris J., the Fobare family, the Foster family, the Garmon sisters, Haydon M., James F., Jaya H., Jessica S., John M., Judd C., Kim & Mars, Kelsey C., Laura A., Leo B., LG Beavers, Libby T., Logan B., Luis R., Luna I., Maddie M., Marc G., Marta F., Matthias W., Mataya E., the McKenna-Lok family, Michael C., Moira C., Piper N., Renée M., Sam T., Samantha W., Scarlet J., Spencer E., Sugar R., Tasha C., Thor & Freya, Travis O., the Trundy family, and the Woodbury family.

Thank you for reading my books. I hope you enjoyed them. Please be a guardian of the forest and a sentinel of the ocean. Page and Molly love you; go rescue a dog!

TO STAY UP-TO-DATE,
CHECK OUT THE WORLD OF

WILD RESCUERS

ONLINE!